SCARLET RAIN

THE ESCAPED
BOOK TWO

KRISTIN CAST

DIVERSIONBOOKS

Also by Kristin Cast

The Escaped Series
Amber Smoke

Diversion Books
A Division of Diversion Publishing Corp.
443 Park Avenue South, Suite 1008
New York, New York 10016
www.DiversionBooks.com

For more information, email info@diversionbooks.com

First Diversion Books edition May 2016.
Print ISBN: 978-1-62681-895-8
eBook ISBN: 978-1-62681-894-1

To Meredith
I aspire to live my life as you do, squeezing every ounce
of joy and adventure out of each moment.

ONE

Robyn Jenkins navigated her sparkling Mercedes through the stop-and-go traffic of Twenty-First Street and breathed a short sigh of relief when she turned onto Terwilleger Boulevard. The quiet, familiar street of the posh Terwilleger Heights neighborhood relaxed her. She unclenched her grip on the steering wheel. The sun always shone brighter in the neighborhood. *Her* neighborhood. As if its halcyon rays knew the residents paid millions to live within blocks of the most beautiful park, museum, and shopping area in midtown Tulsa.

Robyn relaxed her foot on the gas and swiveled her head from one manicured lawn to another. She guided her Mercedes through the craggy shadows cast by the large homes, and silently reminded herself to call her travel agent. The speakers trilled, and she cast an annoyed glance at the unknown number on the dashboard's caller ID.

Perturbed, she punched the answer button on the steering wheel and gathered herself for a moment before chiming, "Hello, this is Robyn."

"Hi, Robyn. It's Elise." She paused. "Elise Cunningham."

Robyn frowned. "Yes, Elise, I know who you are. What can I do for you?"

"I just wanted to run something by you about possibly allowing children at this year's event. What do you think?" she blurted.

Robyn made an effort to keep the bitchiness out of her voice. "I think if something isn't broken, it doesn't need to be fixed."

"So, you're saying you'll consider it then?"

"No, Elise, that's not what I'm saying." Robyn paused to check the status of her coral lipstick in the rearview mirror before continuing. "What I'm saying is that children should *not* be allowed to attend. Period."

"But what if we provide childcare?" Elise's chipper voice bounced through the car, and Robyn jabbed blindly at the volume control. "You asked me to figure out ways to boost ticket sales, and I think we'd have a lot more attendees if they didn't have to find a sitter."

A cringe twisted Robyn's face as she imaged how a room full of squealing children would ruin her perfect event-planning record. "The fundraiser is on the same night every year, and seats start at five hundred dollars. I don't think the attendees will have a hard time finding someone to watch their kids. They must have known something like this would pop up when they decided to procreate. Most of them have live-in help."

"Yes, but—"

"Elise, I hate to stop you, but I just arrived at Monica's. I'll fill her in on your suggestion, and we'll give you a call if we have any questions. Talk soon." She pressed the end call button on her phone, turned off the car, and let out an exhausted breath. She unplugged her phone from the charging station, and carefully slid it into her bag before checking her wrinkleless complexion and hopping out of the car. Her Valentino boots clomped heavily on the stained concrete as she walked toward the open garage. A chill swirled through her appropriately snug cardigan set. "Fall is coming early this year," she murmured, leaning down to touch the swollen chrysanthemum buds. Envy nipped at her thoughts as she admired her friend's tasteful gardening choices. Ivy crept along the house's burgundy brick facade, and hydrangeas held onto their puffy blue flowers. She paused outside of the garage to reassemble herself, smiled widely to cover the jealousy blooming pink in her cheeks, and entered the house.

"Monica, you're not going to believe what Elise suggested." She snickered as she closed the heavy door behind her. "Oh, and the garage door was up, so I let myself in. I didn't think you'd mind." Crisp, clean linen lightly scented the air as she walked through the laundry room and into the expansive kitchen.

She shrugged off her purse strap and clutched the designer bag, taking inventory of the kitchen island before deciding it was best to keep the Birkin on her person. "I see Muriel isn't cleaning today." She bit the inside of her cheek to halt the smirk from painting her face. "There's red pepper all over the counter. You should really do what I do and hire someone to cook. I'll have to give you my chef's number. He'll make your life so much easier." Robyn hooked her purse back over her shoulder and walked to the cabinet she knew held the polished crystal. "It's not too early for wine, I hope." Paper towels bunched under her feet as she clomped toward the wine fridge. "Ugh. This place is disgusting," she grumbled under her breath, kicking away the crumpled paper with the toe of her leather boot. Red glared up at her from the center of the crinkled white. She set down the glasses and carefully squatted next to the wad of towels. Pinching the rough paper between her thumb and forefinger, she narrowed her gaze and brought the towels closer to her face. "Gross," she snipped, flinging the crumpled mass. "Monica, you just have to face it. Cooking is not for you. I mean, *I've* never cut myself in the kitchen, but it is a common occurrence." She reached into the wine fridge and chose the prettiest bottle of red. "You do want a glass of wine, right?" The house remained silent as she waited for an answer.

"Monica, can you hear me?" She filled her own glass and took a sip. She clucked to herself. "This is why two people don't need such a gigantic house. It's amazing they're ever even able to find each other." She left the bottle on the counter and stepped into the living room. Scarlet droplets popped against the pale hardwood, and Robyn followed them hesitantly. "Monica, are you here? Is everything okay?"

She followed the wide hallway and stopped abruptly in the entryway. The beads of blood steadily grew and mixed with tufts of dark hair the closer they got to the stairs. Her breath quickened as she gingerly navigated around the brunette clumps. "Monica? Tyson?" She set a trembling foot on the first stair and silently prayed for someone to pop out and yell "Surprise!"

She took the stairs one at a time, clutching her purse

and making sure of her footing before continuing to the next blood-spattered step. Halfway to the second floor, she nervously called out for her friend. "Monica? Are you up there?" Again, no answer. She reached the top of the staircase, and her gaze followed the lines of red streaking the plush, white carpet leading to the open door of the master bedroom.

She shrieked.

TWO

Dismay clogged Eva's senses, and she twitched wildly against the soft bedding as her final memory dominated her dreams. *"Don't come any closer! I will shoot you, Eva. Don't think I won't."*

She longed to rewind the days. To go back to the understanding man who'd been in her hospital room and promised to help. *"Why are you pointing that at me?"* Pressure thumped within her chest, trapping her voice in her throat. She hacked out her words in choppy, ragged breaths. *"I haven't done anything."* She balled her hands into fists and stepped forward.

"I said, don't come any closer!" The gun shifted as he tightened his grip.

She leaned away from the invisible force tied to the tension consuming her chest. It tugged her backward, toward Alek. Toward where his body had been. She tightened her muscles and forced her legs to move her forward. *"Detective, listen to me."* A pop like gunfire rocketed through Mohawk Park. Then an aching warmth unleashed itself within her core.

"No!" Eva's eyelids flew open. She kicked off the sweltering mound of blankets, and wiped the sweat from her face.

"I'm alive," she whispered. Her eyes adjusted to the dark. Small, neon yellow balls of light came into focus. She patted her torso and leaned back against the pillows. Adrenaline continued to pulse beneath her tingling skin, and her thoughts swirled chaotically in her head. *I'm alive. I'm alive. But what about Alek? Where's Alek?*

She wiped the sleep from her eyes and took inventory of her surroundings. The only light came from glowing orbs in small crystal bowls. They illuminated giant, icicle-shaped formations that filled the room, jutting out from the rocky ceiling and floor like rotten, wet teeth.

She crawled to the side of the bed and placed her feet on the cold stone floor. "Alek?" She stood, her heartbeat quickening. Cool silk brushed against her shins, and she looked down at the long, lavender nightgown fitted snugly against her curvy frame.

"This is seriously not happening to me again."

She bent over and picked up the closest glowing glass bowl. Electricity arced from her hand and bit at her fingertips. "Ouch, jeez." She shook out her right hand while balancing the glass in the other. Blowing on the tips of her stinging fingers, she slowly walked out of the room and into the dark hall.

"Hello? Alek?" The words circled around her and reverberated off the barren rock walls. Eva hunched over the bowl, her hands trembling slightly as she inched her way through the dark. Fear unfurled in her stomach, releasing tendrils of panic and doubt.

"Wait a second. This is ridiculous." Eva righted her posture and shook away the uncertainty. The abrupt movement sent the glowing orb rolling around the bottom of the crystal, causing Eva's stretched shadow to hop from wall to wall. "I've frickin' died. I can handle a creepy, black cave place." She suppressed the last remnants of familiar anxiety and confidently put one foot in front of the other. She said to her echo, "I *am* the Oracle. That should count for something, right?" The echo faded as the hall widened into a large, dimly lit cavern. Eva paused by a linebacker-sized stalagmite and strained to see into the shadowy opening.

A harsh voice bit through the silence. "Maiden, what have you done, bringing the Oracle here?"

Eva peered out from behind the pillar as a second voice emerged.

"I had no choice," Maiden insisted. "I did what was necessary. Had you a heart capable of love, you would have done the same."

"I have a heart, sister," she began, as she lit the first wick on a row of long candles. "But she was in no danger."

"How can you be certain, Mother? You have seen Alek, have you not?"

"I have seen him, yes," she said, her voice softer. She tucked a strand of short, dark hair behind her ear and lit a new match. With each candle lit, the room was illuminated before Eva, revealing the scene. A tall, slender figure emerged from the darkness. Eva clutched the glass against her chest and covered the small beam of light with her fingers.

Maiden stopped abruptly. "Then how can you say she was in no danger? Our son was drained of his power and mere moments from death. We tasked him to save our realm and the mortal realm, and it nearly killed him."

"Their son?" Eva whispered, her breath clouding the inside of the glass bowl. *This is Tartarus. It has to be.*

"If he had listened to me," Maiden snapped, "he would have stayed here longer and had enough energy to safely reach the Oracle, and none of this would have happened."

"If he had listened to *you?*" Mother scoffed and set the matches on a small pedestal near the candles.

"Is it so strange a notion you do not understand its meaning?"

"Maiden, if he had listened to you, he never would have begun training. He would still be suckling at your teat asking for stories of the grand Tartarus of the past." Mother waved her hand dismissively in the air. "Bringing the Oracle here was a foolish decision. One for which we know nothing of the consequences. We are too weak to allow anything we cannot control into our realm."

"Control. That is all you long for. Eva has not even had the chance to discover the basics of her abilities, and we cannot risk losing her. I want to see our home and our son safe. I could not live knowing I could have prevented his death. And what would I say if he awoke to find his Oracle harmed? He would never forgive me."

"He would understand, as I do, that this is not about emotions. Yours or his. This chaos is about the curse you—" Mother stopped short and let out a puff of air.

"Say it, sister. I know it lingers on your tongue."

Mother turned her back on Maiden and walked to the blue stone table at the center of the room. "To what end?"

Maiden uncrossed her arms and quickened her steps to catch up with her sister. "I want to hear from your lips what

I see in your eyes each moment of each day."

Mother gripped the back of one of the silver chairs surrounding the oval table and shook her head.

"Say it!" Maiden cried.

"Sister, end this. It will fix nothing."

"I need to hear you say how this is about the curse *I* caused. Do you think I do not feel the blame suffocating me in this dark hole our home has become?" Maiden choked back tears. "My son's only reason for being is to rebuild what I destroyed. I will never sit idly by and let my past devour him. It has already defined him."

Eva slowly released the breath she'd been holding. The hot air spun around the inside of the glass bowl, fogging it. The ball of greenish light twitched and shook in her hands, and Eva stared at the orb. She yelped, dropping the glass. It shattered on the black stone, and the noise echoed throughout the cavity. The glowing light twitched on the floor as it recovered from the impact.

"Sorry." Eva hopped over the broken glass and into the grand room. "I just, I woke up and it was dark and so—" She searched for a suitable explanation, but couldn't think of anything to explain why she'd been hiding around the corner holding a fat, glowing bug. "I'm just." She took a deep breath and let it out quickly. "I'm sorry."

"You do not need to explain." Maiden smiled and held out her hand. "Come. Join us."

"Eva, I presume," Mother said, more to Maiden than Eva.

"Yes, that's I—or, me." She bowed clumsily. "Sorry, I've never practiced curtseying before now."

"You are the Oracle. There is no need to apologize for

your actions," Mother instructed. "Nor do you need to do that odd motion again."

"Yes, I'm sorry," Eva said without thinking. "No, I'm not sorry. But I am. Just a little. I didn't mean to break your glass or squish your bug."

"Calm yourself Eva, and regain control. You are amongst allies," Mother said flatly.

"More importantly, you are amongst friends." Maiden cast an annoyed glance in Mother's direction.

"You're Alek's moms, right? Is he okay?"

"He was close to death, but he is strong and will find his way out of the dark. He only needs time to heal, and time for our home to replenish all he lost," Mother said.

"If I would've known he was going to use up all of his power to find me, I never would have left Bridget's house. I didn't mean for any of this to happen."

"No one blames you. The choices Alek makes are his own. He also knows how important you are. To our world and yours." A comforting grin lifted the corner of Maiden's eyes.

"He kept saying that, but I don't know how I'm supposed to help. If it wasn't for you, I'd be in jail right now, and I don't even want to think about what would have happened to Alek." Eva's voice trailed off as she remembered him in the park. Bloody, the vibrancy fading from his eyes.

"You need not worry. It will take time, but you will learn how to be a strong and powerful Oracle," Maiden said.

"Time?" Mother sneered. "She says the word as if there is not a curse and a multitude of evil pressing down upon us. You do not have the time to learn. You must search within yourself and find your power. If not—"

"I know, I know," Eva interrupted. "All the freed evil will take over and the world will end and people will die and it'll all be my fault."

Mother's thin lips curled into a half smile. "I see our Alek informed you well. So you know you should be on your way back, to continue vanquishing the evil and restoring our realms."

"What, now? No, no, no. I can't go back now. Alek isn't even healed yet."

"There will be many times when he is unable to join you. You witnessed firsthand what will occur if he is kept in the Mortal Realm for too long and drained of his power," Mother said.

"Well, yeah, but I don't really think my first solo mission should also be my first *mission* mission. I died when I met my first bad guy. And, I was hiding from the police when all that stuff happened with Alek. I don't know if you know what that means, but they're not even half as scary as some crazy evil spirit. I can't go back by myself. Plus, I wouldn't even know how to find a demon-creature thing." She turned to Maiden and pleaded, "Can't I stay here for a little bit longer? Please, I don't have anywhere else to go."

"But what of your family?" Mother asked. "Are you not concerned for them?"

Guilt and sadness rushed through her chest. "Oh, God. My mom. And Bridget. They must be so worried about me, especially my mom." Her shoulders slumped.

"Pay my sister no mind. Your family will be safe in your absence. Just as they were before you awoke as the new Oracle. No need to worry." Maiden rested her hand comfortingly on Eva's back. "You may stay with us until

Alek is fully recovered and able to accompany you on your journey back to the Mortal Realm."

Mother opened her mouth to speak, but closed it just as quickly.

"Something on your mind, sister?" Maiden asked.

"No. I know Alek will heal quickly, and I will take this opportunity to follow your direction."

"Thank you both. Um, I'm not exactly sure what to call you," Eva said.

"You may call us Furies, or by our individual names. Whichever you wish," Maiden replied.

"Isn't there one more of you? I thought Alek said he had three moms."

"Crone, our eldest sister, is keeping watch over Alek," Mother said.

"Can we go see him?" Eva asked.

"He has been through quite a lot. I think it is best for him to rest and regain his strength," Mother advised.

"Please? I've been so worried about him."

Mother's brow wrinkled and her gaze narrowed. "He cannot afford to have any distractions."

"Sister, I am sure you have much to attend to. Oracle, come with me. I will show you around our home." Maiden hooked her arm though Eva's and briskly pulled her away from the table.

"Thank you for being so nice to me, and for rescuing me from your sister," Eva said as soon as they were out of Mother's range of hearing. "I really don't think she likes me."

"Do not let her sour disposition affect you. It has already affected her enough."

"What can I do to get her to warm up to me? I don't

think it'll help, her being so tense all the time."

"I wish I could tell you that feeling would change, but I do not know anymore if that is so. A lot has happened. Mother has become trapped by her bitterness. At times, it seems unending."

Sadness crept onto Maiden's face, and Eva searched for something to lift the mood. "But you seem to be handling this curse thing pretty well. I mean, you don't look a day over twenty-five."

"One's outward appearance does not always convey what has formed inside," Maiden explained, her smile returning. "In comparison to my sisters, I am young. However, I am a different being than you. Even with the new life you now possess. We can discuss this at greater length, but first I must show you one of our greatest assets, which you are fighting to protect."

Maiden led her through a dark opening. Fat balls of light wriggled on the floor. Eva hesitated behind her guide. "I don't want to step on any of your little worm guys."

"All creatures serve a purpose, and all life must end. Come," Maiden said, ushering her deeper into the blackness.

They rounded a corner, and Eva's eyes focused on the only source of light in unending dark. Majestic sapphire waters undulated rhythmically and cast wide beams of turquoise light from a raised basin in the center of the room.

"It's beautiful," Eva whispered.

"It is. However, it is not why I brought you here. This, the Hall of Echoes, was once vibrant and full of life. Out of all of the magics we possess, this room contains the most important." Maiden stepped to the side and glanced down. A pothole-sized puddle glimmered on the charcoal floor.

"What is it?" Eva asked, kneeling next to the pool.

"It is how I knew to save Alek, and how we monitor the happenings of the Mortal Realm. It is also how we are able to protect ourselves from the loosed evils seeking vengeance upon us."

"How many more of these are there?"

"We used to have many. Now, this is all that remains."

"What will happen if this one disappears too?"

"Without these pools, *this* pool, we would be left blind. If we were attacked, the outcome would be the same as if you and Alek failed in your missions."

"The rest of the bad guys would be free," Eva murmured.

"Yes."

"We have to figure out how to put them back before it's too late."

"Every time you and Alek return one of the creatures that escaped to its place within Tartarus's jail, life surges through the Underworld. Restore another evil to its place in our dungeon, and you will also restore Tartarus."

Eva stared at the calm water and asked, "It'll show you anything you want to see?"

"A simple way to put it, but, yes." Maiden squatted next to her and placed her hand over Eva's. "Think of who you most want a vision of. Can you see the person clearly in your mind?"

Eva nodded.

"Good. Now, do not lose focus." Maiden lifted Eva's hand and swirled both of their fingertips in the cool water. Color burst to the surface and an image rippled into place.

"Mom." Tears flooded Eva's eyes and rushed down her cheeks as Lori's soft features came into focus. "I miss her so much. This is the longest I've gone without talking to her. As soon as I get back, I'm going to fix this. All of it."

"You need not be saddened." Maiden tilted Eva's chin so their eyes met. "Within you is the power to regain control and finally put an end to this curse."

"You think so?"

"I know. In time, you will too. Now, let us move to something more joyful, yes?"

Eva wiped her eyes and let Maiden guide her to her feet.

"There is something I have dreamed of showing to someone other than my sisters. They cannot appreciate this, as I know you will. Would you like to see it?"

Eva shrugged as she dried the last of her tears from her cheeks. "As long as it's not scary or stinky."

Maiden again looped her arm through Eva's and directed her back into the dark. "I assure you, it is neither. Although, you just might die."

Eva stiffened as she thought of all of the possible creatures and lamenting spirits Tartarus might house. Tempering her uneasiness, she let Maiden guide her further into the twisting black of Tartarus.

THREE

James sat at his desk, absentmindedly clicking the end of his pen, staring blankly at the computer screen. *She was there. Right in front of me. And then she was gone. Vanished. Poof.* He replayed the moments in Mohawk Park before Eva's disappearance. *People don't just disappear.* He clicked the pen a few more times. *I aimed my gun. Told her not to come any closer. Then there was that noise. And the smell, like something burning.*

The double doors leading into the front of the station flew open. Their etched-glass panels rattled, jerking James from his thoughts.

"Ma'am! Ma'am! You can't go back there!" A young officer jogged down the hall, calling after the woman who'd stormed through the doors.

"Lori Kostas?" James's brow furrowed as he searched his memory for a scheduled meeting he may have missed.

Her gaze swept the room, and settled on James. "Detective Graham, I need to talk to you," she shouted.

"Sorry, Detective," the officer apologized. Lori planted

herself in the empty chair next to James's desk. "I told her to wait and that I'd come get you, but—"

"But I'm tired of waiting, Detective," Lori interjected. "I need answers. I couldn't sit by the phone for another second hoping you would call with some sort of news."

"Thank you." James read the officer's name badge. "Thank you Blevins. I'll take it from here."

Blevins nodded and quickly made his way back to his post.

"I apologize for barging in on you like this. It's not what I would normally do, not that any of what's going on falls under the "normal" heading, but I had to do something. Waiting around for answers while I imagine my own version of what's happening is making me feel crazy." Lori's eyes swelled with tears. "Do you know anything new?"

He shook his head somberly. "I wish there was something I could tell you, but there haven't been any new developments in your daughter's case."

"But you still think Eva's a part of this?" She leaned forward and lowered her voice. "That she and Bill and that other man killed that young woman and are now on the run?"

"At this time, we're investigating every possible angle."

"Don't give me that bullshit." Spittle flew from her mouth as anger chopped her words. "You were there the night she was found. You talked to her at the hospital. Do *you* believe she's guilty?"

Fear and sadness had leached into Eva's voice. *Please, just give me a chance to explain.* It stained his memory and made him question what he thought he understood about the case, and Eva's guilt.

"Ms. Kostas, there are a lot of unanswered questions about what's going on. At this point, I can't tell you whether or not I think she's guilty." His gaze drifted down to the buffed white tile between his feet. "There are strange things happening. Right now I don't know what to believe."

"Excuse me, Detective."

James cleared his throat. "Blevins, everything is good here. Thanks for checking."

"The captain sent me to find you. He wants to see you and your partner in his office. I already talked to Detective Schilling. He's on his way there now."

James stood and shuffled papers around on his desk, avoiding eye contact with Lori. "I'm sorry to cut this short. I have to get in there."

"Please let know me as soon as you find something out." Lori placed her hand on his shoulder and squeezed it gently. "I appreciate your honesty, Detective. Even though it wasn't exactly what I wanted to hear, it's the only real answer I've gotten. Thank you."

James continued rearranging the same stack of papers until Lori exited through the double doors. "Get your head together, James." He balled his hands into fists and pressed them against the surface of his desk. "There's an explanation for all of this. Work the case. Find out what happened." He took a few deep breaths, and straightened his posture before heading toward the captain's office.

The door to Captain Alvarez's office was closed, and James stood outside of it, staring at his reflection in the engraved gold placard. "Tell him what happened exactly as you wrote it in the report." He rolled his neck a few times and rubbed at the tension sprouting in his shoulders. "It's simple. Stick to the story." James knocked rapidly before cracking the door and poking his head into the office. "You wanted to see me?"

"Come in. Take a seat," Captain Alvarez said, running a hand through his thinning hair. The fluorescent lighting glinting off of his scalp and forehead made him appear to wear a permanent layer of sweat.

"Sorry I'm late. Lori Kostas came and insisted I talk to her." He settled into the only available chair next to Schilling.

Captain Alvarez pursed his lips. "She have any new information on the whereabouts of any of the suspects?"

"No, she has no idea. More than anything, she's freaked out and wants her daughter home."

"What I'd like to know more than anything is how she was able to get away from us. For a second time. Her daughter, that is," Schilling huffed.

"So would I," James mumbled, picking at a few loose threads on the cuff of his shirt.

"You have something to say, Graham?" Alvarez opened his desk drawer and pulled out a manila envelope stuffed with papers.

"Nothing, sir. Just agreeing with Schilling."

Alvarez dropped the thick packet on his desk and started thumbing through its contents. "But you were there for her second disappearance, were you not?"

"Yes sir I was. It's all in my report."

"I read your report, and all the others associated with this case. They're right here, actually." He poked the file with his index finger. "But I'd like to hear it from you."

James grabbed the chair's armrests to keep from fidgeting in his seat. "Yes sir. There was a loud noise, and when—"

"No, I want to hear it from the beginning. When you first arrived on scene." Alvarez leaned back in his chair. *Repeat what you wrote in the report. What you saw didn't happen. It couldn't have. There's an explanation. Get through this, then find it.* His heart fluttered with his increasing nerves. "Fine. From the beginning." He gripped the armrests so tightly the color drained from his knuckles.

A shrill ring erupted from the captain's phone, and he glanced down at its screen. "Give me a second." He answered the phone, and spun around in his chair.

Schilling leaned over and whispered, his stale-coffee breath coating each word, "It's shit, but what are you gonna do?"

"Hmm? Sorry, I wasn't paying attention. Got a lot going on."

"Relax, Graham. Fuckups happen." James kept his expression blank as Schilling searched his face. "You losing Eva. It *was* just a fuckup, right?"

Alvarez's chair turned, and he dropped his phone back on the desk. "Where were we? Oh, yeah, the beginning. Go ahead, Graham."

James shook away his nerves and thought back to what he'd written in his report. "Schilling and I entered the Mohawk Park trail from the east. Shortly after, it forked, and we separated. I took the path on the left, and Schilling went to the right. I heard what I thought were the sounds of a male and a female talking, and I followed their voices."

"So you thought you heard a male and a female, but that wasn't the case?" Alvarez asked.

James kept his gaze fixed on the captain and continued with his version of events. "When I turned the corner, one of the suspects, Eva Kostas, was there alone. She was covered in blood. I could not determine from my visual whether any or all of it was her own. I asked her if Alek was with her. She said he'd disappeared, and that she needed my help to find him. I assumed, because of the voices I'd heard, that Alek had to be nearby."

James fidgeted as Alvarez jotted a few notes down on a piece of paper. "Did she say anything else about his location other than needing your help to find him?"

"No, just that he was gone. She then proceeded to approach me. At which time, I raised my weapon and warned her not to come any closer. Then there was a loud noise. It sounded like a gunshot."

"I heard it too, Captain," Schilling added. "The trail I was on looped back around. By that time, I wasn't too far from Graham."

"The noise, I thought Schilling was firing. Maybe Alek had found him and he was in trouble. It distracted me. I turned to find the source of the sound, and see if Schilling needed help. When I turned back around, Eva was gone. She must have run off. I looked, but didn't find any sign of her."

"Okay." Alvarez nodded to himself as he wrote down a few final notes. "You served overseas, right Graham?"

"Yes sir. I served one tour in Iraq with the Forty-Fifth Infantry Division."

Alvarez set his pen down and folded his fingers together. "There a lot of noise over there? Gunshots, explosives?"

James's brow lowered as he stared across the desk at the captain. "Is there something you're trying to get at, Captain?"

Alvarez shook his head. "Not at all. I just want to see where your head was at."

"My head was in the case. In that moment. I heard something that sounded like a gun and I wanted to make sure my partner didn't need me." James hovered between sitting and standing. "I didn't let her go. I don't know where she is."

"I don't think you turned your back and let one of our main suspects walk off. But you need to understand that this shit show is all our city is talking about. It's the top story on every goddamn news station in the state. When David called me about you, I didn't hesitate in giving you a position here. I go way back with his family. His daughter was like my own, and when she passed, it hurt me just as bad as you." He paused a moment. "The department can't afford any more mistakes. Don't make me regret doing you a favor. You got me?"

"Yes, sir," James said, lowering himself back into his chair.

"Now." Alvarez adjusted his tie and smoothed his wispy hair. "I'm assuming, since both of you were available to come into my office for this little sit down, that there are no new leads."

Schilling cleared his throat before speaking. "We've got their pictures plastered everywhere and on every news outlet. All three of them: Eva Kostas, Bill Morgan, and Alek Whoever-the-fuck. But nothing so far."

"This Alek character. We still don't know anything about him? Haven't found him in any database?" Alvarez asked.

"We haven't even been able to figure out his last name," Schilling muttered.

"Nothing has popped. No one's ever heard of him. He's a complete mystery," James said.

"This whole fucking case is a mystery. Evidence that

leads nowhere, suspects disappearing—it's a nightmare," Schilling said.

"Which is why, gentlemen, we're putting this one on the back burner."

"What? There have to be more leads we can check out, something we can do. There are way too many unanswered questions. You can't take this away from us," James pleaded.

"No one's taking anything away from anybody. Just pushing it to the side while we wait for something new to hit. Those kids can't stay gone for long. They'll need money, someplace to stay. They'll surface soon. In the meantime, I can't have you two spending all your time chasing your tails. Whether we like it or not, other murders do happen in this town, and the public needs to feel safe. Plus, we're in hot water with the press, and I've got to get my ass out before it starts boiling."

"What'll you have us do while everything cools off?" Schilling asked, scratching his swollen belly.

"I'm sending you out on something new. It's in Terwilleger Heights." Alvarez smirked.

"This should be good," Schilling chuckled.

"Why?" James looked back and forth between the two men. "What's Terwilleger Heights?"

"Land of Daddy Warbucks. The cases that come out of there would make that Real Housewives bullshit look like a day in Disneyland. It's all lots of unnecessary hoity-toity frou-frou drama if you ask me," Schilling said, his Okie twang stretching his words. "Let me guess, some pool boy got whacked in the back of the head with a gold-plated vase after the husband caught him cleaning his wife's pipes?"

"Not quite," Alvarez chuckled.

"The wife caught the husband with the pool boy?"

"Don't think that's quite the story, but that's what you two are paid to figure out." He reached into his desk, took out another file, and held it out to Schilling. "Winslow's already out there. He'll fill you in when you arrive."

"Thanks, Captain." Schilling took the file and stuffed it under his arm. "We'll get this one taken care of."

James lifted himself from the chair, and nodded in the captain's direction before heading toward the door. "Sounds like we should be able to button this one up pretty quick." James exhaled for what felt like the first time since he'd sat down across from Alvarez.

"We might just get you home in time to get caught up on some of that beauty rest you so desperately need. You're looking like shit." Schilling adjusted the file under his arm and unclipped his keys from his belt loop. "You going to explain what happened in there, or am I going to have to force it out of you?"

"What do you mean?" James asked, waving to a group of officers as he and Schilling passed by.

"You know what I mean. You blowing up at the captain, and all that stuff about him doing you a favor and someone dying. You're lucky all you got was a warning. I've seen him shove that size-fourteen boot up an ass or two. It ain't pretty. You might not be so lucky next time you decide to pop off."

"He didn't do *me* any favors, and I didn't '*pop off*,'" James mocked Schilling's hick accent. "Look, I don't want to talk about it. We should do what the captain said and put the whole case on the back burner. We'll talk about it again when we get a new lead."

Schilling pushed open the door to the parking lot and

stepped onto the sun-soaked concrete. "Shit, boy. There's no reason to get all fired up. I've been by your side the whole way, and you're not going to blow me off now. Rookie mistake number twelve."

"Stop it with the rookie mistake bullshit. I earned my badge, same as you. I'm not some kid. I deserve to be here."

Schilling stopped at his car and locked his gaze on his partner. "Something happened out there in those woods that you're not telling me."

James threw his hands in the air and shook his head. "It happened just like I said in there and in my report. You think I'm lying?"

"I think whatever it is has got you so fucking scared you'd rather blow up everything around you than actually deal with what's going on."

"What are you now, some kind of psychiatrist?" James nervously ran his fingers through the back of his hair. "You know what? I'm not doing this. I'll get the address from dispatch and meet you there."

"Bullshit you will. We're going to get in the car, and you're going to deal with this like a man." Schilling pressed the key fob and opened the driver's side door. "I can't have a partner who's lying and doesn't trust me."

"Schilling, if that's the way you feel, then maybe we shouldn't be partners." James abruptly turned, and silently cursed to himself as he jetted back into the station. He knew his partner was right, dammit.

Four

Cal slumped against the back of the bench and glared at the three dots glowing up at her from the screen of her phone. "Come on, Kevin. Whatever you have to say shouldn't take this long."

The phone chirped as his message finally came through. *Class got out late. Be there soon.*

"Of course it did." She sighed and punched in a reply. *Hurry! The bus will be here any minute.*

The screen darkened as she again waited for the three blinking dots to reveal a message.

Down the street. Pedaling fast. Make them wait.

She huffed and tucked her phone into the side pocket of her tote bag.

A few minutes early, the bright green Tulsa Transit bus pulled up to the stop and let out a sharp hiss as it settled into park. The accordion-style door folded open, and the gaunt driver offered Cal his best smile.

"Afternoon." He tipped an invisible hat and gnawed at

the wad of gum in his mouth.

"Sorry to ask you to do this, but could you wait just a few minutes? My boyfriend is only a few blocks away." Cal grinned at the driver and slipped her EZ Ride pass in the fare box. "But he's riding his bike, so it shouldn't take too much longer."

The driver adjusted his crisp blue shirt and flicked his glance to the large rearview mirror. "I am a little early. But we're almost completely full, so I'm only givin' him another couple of minutes. Gotta get these people to their stops on time."

"Thank you so much. That's plenty of time. He'll be here." Cal stepped back out onto the sidewalk and shielded her eyes against the sun as she looked up the street in the direction of the community college. "There he is! Just at the intersection." She pointed. "Can't miss that bright orange OKC Thunder hat."

"I see him. I see him."

"Kev! Come on!" she shouted, and waved for him to hustle.

He lazily waved back, too preoccupied with the strap hanging around his neck to cross the street when the crosswalk signal illuminated.

She put her hands on her hips and impatiently tapped her toe on the sidewalk. Annoyance fluttered in her chest, and she tried her best not to glare at him. "Always so busy messing with that stupid GoPro. I wish he'd just throw it in the garbage."

Muted buzzing hung in the air around Cal. She swung her tote around to the front and dug in the side pocket for her phone. "Wouldn't have to call me if you were at the bus stop on time." She yanked out her phone and stared confusedly at her reflection in the black screen.

Brow furrowed, she turned to the driver and asked, "Do you hear that? It sounds like something's vibrating. It might be coming from the bus."

He huffed and cocked his head to the side. "No excuses are going to get me to stay longer. I watched your boyfriend sit through that light. He better start peddlin' next chance he gets or—"

"Wait, shh." Cal craned her neck and listened. "It's louder. You really don't hear that? Your bus sounds like it might be about to break down."

He squinted his eyes, as if narrowing his field of vision would help him to hear. "It's probably the electrical wires. All that juice runnin' through 'em, they're bound to crackle every once in awhile. You can hear 'em humming real good over out by my sister's place."

His long-winded hypothesis faded into the background as she focused on the heightened humming.

A car horn blared as Kevin bailed off his bike and stepped into traffic. Her attention snapped toward the sound of his frantic, muffled shouts.

She put her hands up by her shoulders and shrugged. "I have no idea what you're saying. There's too much traffic noise."

He cupped his hands around his mouth and yelled, "Get on the bus!"

"No, we're waiting for you."

"There's something…."

His shouts were overtaken as the buzzing swirled into a roar.

There's something above you. Each word shot down at her in a shriek like a freshly launched firework.

FIVE

The delicate silk nightgown offered Eva little warmth, and even less protection from whatever was lurking behind the door. She wrapped her arms around her torso and braced herself.

Maiden threw open the door, and gestured for Eva to walk ahead, graciously at first, then impatiently. "What is it that you are waiting for? I invited you in, did I not?"

"You said whatever's in there might kill me. I've already died one too many times. Thanks, but I'm good out here," Eva said, shuffling backward.

Maiden grabbed Eva's arm and pulled her through the doorway. "Is that not a saying in the Mortal Realm? Although you just might die?"

"Yes, but if we're talking about sayings, I prefer 'let's do brunch.'" Eva passed the perplexed Fury and took in the grand, fabulous room. A circle of candles illuminated the space and cast dancing shadows on the high, vaulted ceilings. Mirrors lined one wall, reflecting rows of beautiful dresses and sparkling shoes.

"This is… incredible," she breathed.

"I was certain I used the phrase correctly," Maiden continued. "I had Alek explain its meaning several times in hopes of avoiding any confusion when I used it myself."

"No, you definitely used it right." Eva stepped to the first rack of clothes and brushed her hand through the fabrics. "I just didn't know you knew any of our sayings."

Maiden collapsed on a mound of puffy pillows in the center of the ring of candles. "What do you think?"

"This is crazy. I've never seen anything like this before. It's practically a ballroom. I feel like Belle in the Beast's library. It's amazingly fantastic."

Maiden twirled the ends of her hair and blushed. "After the curse infected our realm, I was confined to a small area of Tartarus. To keep from losing my mind, I started to sew. It was something I learned as a little girl, but had not practiced in decades. It took time for me to become skilled enough to produce what you see before you, but it soothed me and helped the hours pass. It was well worth the work."

"Do you think I'll be like you? Crappy in the beginning, but eventually incredible at what I do?"

"Eva, given enough time and practice, you will be a great and powerful Oracle, like those before you. You must believe in yourself. First, however, we need to find you attire better suited to your title," she said, springing up from the pillows.

"You're going to have to meet my friend someday," Eva said as Maiden sorted through the dresses. "You and Bridget would definitely connect over your gorgeous closets. Although, I'm pretty sure she's never made anything before in her life. We'll have to schedule something for the next time you come up to the Mortal Realm."

Maiden shook her head. "We have never ventured to any realm outside of those in the Underworld."

"Well, you should come visit sometime. I can show you all around Tulsa. It's not as exciting as someplace like New York City, but it sure is different from here. There's a lot more light, for one thing."

"Thank you for the offer. I am sure I would enjoy exploring the Mortal Realm of Tulsa with you, but I cannot."

"Sure, not right now. I mean after everything has settled down, and the curse has been obliterated. I get why you wouldn't want to go on a vacation until after then. Hopefully all this will be over soon," Eva mumbled.

"I cannot go at anytime. I am a part of Tartarus, and it is a part of me. Just as you cannot separate yourself from your body, I cannot separate myself from the Underworld," Maiden explained.

"Then how do you ever meet guys or make any friends?" Eva asked.

"I was in love. Once," she said quietly.

"Really? With who? I love a good love story, but I didn't think I'd hear one in the Underworld."

Maiden dabbed her cheeks with her fingertips.

"Oh, Maiden, I'm sorry. I didn't realize it was a sensitive subject. You don't have to talk about it."

"No, it is fine." She shook her hair away from her face, and took a shaky breath before continuing. "His name is Galen. His soul is sentenced here for an eternity for a crime he did not commit. Although it was forbidden, we fell very much in love." Tears streamed down her face and dotted the delicate gold fabric of her dress. "In all the years of my existence, I have never yearned to be with someone more than I crave to be with Galen."

"What happened? Did he get set free?"

"He remains here. He will remain here until the end of time."

"Then why not go be with him? You said yourself you can travel anywhere down here."

"The curse, our love, is the vessel in which it was created. I cannot imagine what would have become of Tartarus if we had continued our affair."

"Oh, Maiden." She wrapped her arms around the youngest Fury. Citrus and honey scents burst from Maiden's hair. "I'm so sorry. That's awful. After Alek and I have fixed this curse, I'll find a way for you and Galen to be together."

Maiden lifted her head and stepped back. "You would attempt something so kind?"

"Yeah, of course. I'm the Oracle now. It'll be just another way for me to use my powers for good, and what's a better reason than true love? But, now that I think about it, I *will* actually need you to do something for me."

"And what would you have me do?" Maiden asked apprehensively.

"Whenever you go see him, you have to let me help you pick out what to wear."

"I am sure that can be arranged," Maiden said, beaming. "Now, let us find you a spectacular garment."

"I think I already found one." Eva pulled the dress from its hanger and held it up in front of her body.

"It will look lovely on you. You may put it on in here. I can step out if you would like."

"Are you kidding? We're friends now, and we have all the

same girl parts. You don't have to leave. Plus, I'll need your help with the clasps in the back."

The dress felt like water as she pulled it over her head and let the gauzy fabric lap against her legs and flow to the floor. "This color is amazing," she commented, admiring how the orange fabric made her skin appear to be a bit darker. "It reminds me of summer."

"I must have had thoughts of you while making the gown. It is perfect." Maiden smiled.

"Will you take me to see Alek now?" Eva asked as she studied her reflection in the grand mirrors. "I mean, I absolutely love your closet and I can't wait to see Tartarus get back to normal, but I won't stop obsessing about whether or not he's actually going to be okay until I get to see him."

"Last I checked, he was not awake. And Mother, though she was quite rude, did have a point when she said he needs his rest."

"That's okay." Eva turned to face Maiden. "I don't need him to be awake. I won't disturb him. I just need to make sure he's really here and that he's really alive."

Maiden sighed and bit her lip. "Who am I to keep you apart? Yes. Yes, I will take you to him."

"Thank you!" Eva blurted, surprised by her own excitement.

"Follow me. I will lead you to his quarters. However, we cannot enter until Crone has finished her healing ritual, if she has not done so already."

Eva stayed in stride with Maiden as she exited the magnificent closet and walked briskly down the wide hallway. "How long will that take?"

"It is different with each individual. With you it did not

take long, because your injuries were not severe."

"My injuries?" Eva thought back to her time in Mohawk Park. "I might have scraped up my hands and knees, but I wouldn't really call those *injuries*. You make them sound so major."

"Although you did have a few scrapes and bruises, the injuries I speak of were sustained from your travel here. Never before have I, or any one of us, brought a mortal through the void between the realms and into Tartarus."

"Yeah, Alek told me he couldn't bring me here because he'd only brought dead bodies back with him before. Creature dead bodies, not normal human dead bodies."

Maiden smiled. "And he was wise not to try. Although my abilities are more advanced, and I have more control over them than Alek does his, you were not free from danger when I pulled you from the Mortal Realm."

"How did you know coming here wouldn't kill me?" Eva asked.

"I had to accept the risk. I knew my son was dying and I assumed the worst would happen to you. Luckily, it did not. You only suffered a few minor burns from the abundance of energy created when traveling through realms. With your ability to heal, and Crone's ability to assist with that process, you were restored to health quite quickly. The only reason you slept for as long as you did was because coming here was a great shock to your system, and understandably so."

"Wait, you know that I can heal myself?"

Maiden nodded. "It was something Crone discovered when she was working on you, but I was not surprised. I know it is an ability possessed by many of the Oracles who came before you."

"Did Crone discover anything else? Any other abilities?" Eva asked, trying to still her anticipation.

"You do not yet know what other powers you possess?"

"Well, no. That's why I'm asking you. Why? Am I supposed to know already? Is that something I missed?"

Maiden chuckled. "Remain calm, Eva. Most abilities come in threes. There are some exceptions to this rule, but I do not believe you fit into any of those."

"So you're saying I have two other abilities I know nothing about?"

"Perhaps. And perhaps, in time, they will come."

"But what if I want them now? What if I *need* them now, for the next bad thing that's running loose? How do I speed up the discovery process? I need all the help I can get, and it kind of freaks me out that these abilities are just sitting inside of me, waiting to pop up at any time."

"If you were newly birthed, would you expect to walk?" Maiden asked. "Even though you are in the same body with the same memories, part of you is new to this world. Have trust and be patient. Give yourself time to grow and mature."

"Oh my God. This is like going through puberty all over again," Eva groaned. "At least I won't be shoved in an institution that bases your social worth on where you sit at lunch."

Maiden looked at her, puzzled.

"Never mind. Can I ask you a question?" Eva continued, "It's probably going to sound really stupid, but I was just thinking about how much I loathed high school. I always thought I'd go back to our ten-year reunion and have this amazing career and husband, and all this other stuff I could rub in people's faces. Now I don't see any of that happening.

I know you said I'm new to this world, or at least part of me is, but does that mean I have to completely change who I am?"

Maiden stopped in front of a large door identical to the one they had just exited. "I am afraid, young Oracle, that is a question to which only you can find the answer."

"It's just, I really liked the old me, and now I don't feel like I know who I'm supposed to be. The more I think about everything that's going on, the more I don't think I can do this. A week ago, I didn't know this place existed, and my biggest worry was that I'd end up being some lonely old spinster who still lived with her mom. I don't know anything about anything that's going on now. What's worse is that, if I mess up, a lot of people will die. I bet they'd all be super pissed if they knew I was half of the team that was supposed to keep the world from ending." She leaned her back against the wall, and slid down to the floor. "Go team," she said, lifting her arm in the air listlessly.

"You are being too hard on yourself. I am impressed with how you have handled all that has been put in your path. There is a lesson I learned many years ago. One which, I am sorry to say, I have not been practicing as I should. However, it did help me when I had the sense to use it. Would you like to know what it is?"

"Of course! I'd love to learn some kind of magic." Eva stifled the urge to hop up and down like she'd just received an invitation to Hogwarts.

"No, Eva, it is not magic that I speak of. At least, not the kind of which you are thinking. This power is within us all, and is the simplest gift you can give yourself. Kindness."

"Kindness? I already try not to be mean to anyone. Sure,

a lot of people out there could use a refresher course, but I don't see how that's giving myself a gift, or how it's supposed to help me sort this out."

"What would it be like if the person you spent the most time with always judged and criticized your actions, your appearance, your likes and dislikes?"

"I'm sure it would suck really bad, but they also wouldn't be in my life for long."

"Precisely. If you would not allow another person to treat you so cruelly, why then do you do it to yourself? Be kind to yourself and mirror that kindness in your thoughts. After all, your thoughts are with you always. Change them, and you change your world."

"I'm pretty sure I've seen that on a magnet somewhere."

The door opened, and Crone emerged from the dimly lit room. "It is nice to see you up and well."

"Maiden told me about what you did when I arrived. I want to thank you for helping me, so thank you." She curtsied sloppily.

"It was an honor to assist the new Oracle." Crone nodded respectfully as shadows slipped into the deep creases nestled around her smile.

"How is our son?" Maiden asked.

"Much improved. It should not be long now before he is again on his feet and causing trouble."

"Can I see him?" Eva asked.

"He would welcome your visit more than that of any one of his mothers. Now, I must retire. This day has taken much out of me." Soothing scents of sage and wet earth drifted from her skin as she brushed passed Eva and disappeared down the dark hall.

Eva nervously approached the open door. "I can go in now, right?"

"Whenever you wish."

Flickering candlelight cast dizzying shadows around the room. A tall mirror, a large wardrobe, and an empty shelf were the only items in the undecorated space. "Alek." Eva rushed to him and stood motionless at his bedside. A thick, white bandage wrapped around his thigh, protecting the huge gash he'd suffered in the Mortal Realm. "Crone is sure he'll wake up soon?" she asked, studying his face. His skin was flushed and dotted with sweat. "That wound on his leg was really bad."

"It is not his bodily injuries which worry me. Alek is not only his body, just as you are not only yours. His body will heal. The worry I have for him is the same he had for you before you awoke as the new Oracle."

"What are you worried about? What could happen to him?"

"Alek, with Pythia's aid, contacted you in the dream world so you would not be lost there. Now we can only wait and hope he finds his way back to us, just as you found your way back to him."

Carefully, Eva sat next to him on the bed. "Alek, please." She took his hand in hers, and a spark of electricity crackled between their palms. "Ouch, dammit." She dropped his hand and shook off the pain. "Why does that keep happening?"

• • •

"Ouch, dammit." Alek dropped his keys and let them slap against the stone steps. He brought his hand closer to his face and inspected the quickly healing burn on his palm. "Strange," he remarked, plucking the keys from the step. Remembering how easily mortal craftsmanship could be destroyed, he unlocked the front door and opened it gently. "Eva," he called, stepping inside and jiggling the key free from the lock. "I've returned."

The house was dark, and the air conditioner hummed steadily though the vents.

"Eva?" He closed the door and quietly hung his keys on the hook. "Are you here?" Concern bubbled in his stomach as he took inventory of the kitchen and living room. Alek quickened his pace as he approached the closed door at the end of the hall. Muscles tensed and ready, he carefully pushed it open. "Eva?"

"Alek, you're back." She poked her head out from under the comforter and yawned.

"You are safe."

"Of course I am. I have you to protect me." Her smile melted the tension rippling in his broad back.

She motioned for him to come to her, and he slipped off his shirt and dove beneath the covers. He left a gentle trail of kisses up her thighs, stomach, and chest before his head broke free of the silky sheets, and his eyes met hers.

"I've missed you." Eva pressed her soft mouth to his. "I didn't think you'd come home to me."

"I will always find you and come back to you. I promise." She smiled against his lips and she wrapped her legs around his waist, lifting her hips toward him. He pressed his body against hers and kissed her hungrily.

"Wait, wait," she whispered. "He's here, and wants to talk to you."

He pulled back, studying her face. "Who? Are you in danger?"

"Shh," Eva pressed her finger against his lips. "Don't act, just listen."

"Warrior of Tartarus," an unassuming voice called.

Alek shot from the bed and faced the slender man leaning against the doorframe. "I will give you one chance to leave unharmed," he growled.

"Relax, Alek." The man took his hands out of the pockets of his tailored pants and held them by his sides. "I'm not here to cause any trouble."

Alek tightened his fists. "How do you know me?"

"I've had a long time to watch you, Tartarus, and the Mortal Realm, and I want to help." He nodded at Eva. "Both of you."

"Who are you?"

"You're stuck here, and until you're free, nothing can move forward." He waved his bony fingers in the air. "All of this—her, this form I've taken—none of it's real. You really messed yourself up on your last excursion to the Mortal Realm. Because of that, you're now trapped in a kind of dream world and, unfortunately for you, you're not strong enough to get out by yourself."

"Let me guess, you are here to lend assistance."

"I am." His eyes were the green of an antique computer screen, and they glimmered when he smiled. "I can call upon someone with enough juice to launch you back into your body."

Alek crossed his arms. "For what price?"

"I knew I'd like you. Didn't I say that I would like him?" He winked at Eva, and she giggled.

"Get on with it," Alek commanded.

"No need to get huffy." He cleared his throat and continued. "There will come a time when I'll ask you a question, and the only thing I'll need you to do is say yes."

"And if I say no?"

"I'm not a fan of veiled threats, and I don't like beginning relationships with dishonesty, so I'll be blunt. If you choose to deny me, I'll slaughter the Furies, then I'll kill your cute little girlfriend over there. Well, the real version of her."

Alek charged forward, but the man evaporated as soon as he made contact.

The air shimmered as he reappeared. "Not a very nice thing to do, Alek. I won't hurt them if I don't have to."

"Tell me who you are." Alek spit out the words from between clenched teeth.

"For now, you can call me H." He brushed clean the sleeves of his suit coat and adjusted his striped tie. "So, do we have a deal?"

Alek's eyes settled on the fake version of Eva. She waved at him gaily, unaffected by H's presence.

"Or, you could choose to stay here with this version of the Oracle. No harm will come to either of you, but in reality, she and Tartarus will both die because of your selfishness, and it'll happen soon."

"I'll do it!" Alek roared and turned to face H. "If any harm comes to them, I'll rip you apart."

H extended his hand, and Alek glared down at his thin fingers. "Say yes when I ask, and I won't kill them. I'm a man of my word, Alek, as I know you are too."

Against his instincts, Alek forced his hand into H's and shook it.

"You're doing the right thing," H reassured. "I'll make sure one of your friends knows of your existence here— anonymously, of course, but she'll still return you to Tartarus. You won't remember meeting me, not until I want you to, but I'm sure it's going to be a pleasure working with you. Talk soon."

Alek blinked, and H was gone. Dull, pulsing pain spread through his forehead, and he massaged his temples.

"Hey, you okay? Come back to bed. It'll make you feel better." Eva shuffled over and patted the open space next to her.

"I feel like there is something important I've forgotten." A blurred memory sat at the front of his mind, and he fought to focus on it through the haze.

Laughter trickled into his ears, and Alek's gaze darted around the room. "Do you hear that? The sound is familiar."

"I hear many things, young immortal," Pythia said, staring up at him with a sultry smile.

Alek recoiled. "Pythia!"

She threw back the sheets to reveal her naked body. "Do I look like another?"

"I—" Alek's gaze roamed her shimmering slopes and stilled on her luscious breasts. Her long, frost-colored hair twirled in an invisible wind.

"Is this not what you have wanted all along, warrior? Me, on my back, giving you permission?" A smooth grin parted her lips as faint laughter flooded his ears.

Alek lifted his gaze to hers and studied her expression. "This is not your true form, only an illusion. I have witnessed what lies beneath," he said, pushing away the memory of her shuddering eyes and rancid mouth. "What have you done with Eva?"

"You do not know?" She chuckled and propped herself on her elbow.

"Know what?" he asked, picking up his shirt.

"I felt you walking lost in this dream world. Your body screaming for the Oracle. Your passion penetrated me and sank into my bones." She closed her eyes and let her fingers wander down the curves of her softly glowing skin. "You have let her cloud your judgment."

"Dream world?" He stuffed his arms into his shirt and threw it on over his head. "I've had this talk before, but cannot remember its end. Bring Eva back to me."

Her gaze locked on his. "You command me? You have not been here long, yet your mind is already betraying you." She stood, her skin pulsing soft amber. "Do you forget the power I possess?"

Alek inched backward as the specter grew nearer. "No, I—"

"Silence!" she commanded with a guttural growl. "The warrior within you is fading, young immortal." She closed her eyes and cocked her head to the side. "Can you hear him? He cries for battle, for vengeance, for blood. He screams and claws within you, yet you do not heed him." Her eyes fluttered open and settled on him. "He pulses through your veins, powering your heart, yet he goes unnoticed. She must accept your heart for her own sanity, but you will never be fully hers. Your true heart, your warrior's heart, is chained to Tartarus. Refuse him, let him die, and what creature will you be?"

Alek stiffened. "I am an immortal warrior of Tartarus. I will avenge my home and save the Mortal Realm."

"Then why do you rot here? This will never be!" Pythia screeched. Her body swelled in size, and her translucent skin ignited into fiery gold.

Amber light poured from her, and Alek shielded his eyes from the glow. "I will never betray my duty," he shouted through her echoing screams.

As quickly as she had become enraged, her color cooled, and she returned to her lithe, elegant form. "Young immortal, I feel your warrior strong within you. This gift is his." She floated toward him and pressed her frosty lips against his forehead. "I will heal your mind. Free you from this illusion." Amber smoke poured from her mouth as she spoke. It blanketed his lips and crept onto his tongue. He felt the gentle smoke seep into his chest, and a refreshing burst of cool energy popped within him. "Now return and fight!"

With Pythia's aid, Alek released his grip and closed his eyes as the room around him melted, claimed by the blackness of sleep.

SIX

A prickling rawness irritated the back of Cal's throat. Her mouth tasted like pennies. "What happened?" She lifted her head off the pavement and rubbed her fingers through her wet, matted hair.

Kevin hovered over her. "Just stay still. You hit your head pretty hard. It knocked you out for a little bit. The bus driver called an ambulance." Worry turned down the corners of his mouth and creased his forehead, and Cal regretted ever being annoyed with him for running late.

"I sure did," the driver said. "It should be here in a jiff. They'll take you to the hospital and get ya all checked out."

"Hey, you closed the door when those bug things were swarming me. That was an asshole move." Her lungs tickled, and she let out a short burst of wet coughs.

"Yeah, man. Not cool at all," Kevin agreed.

"Waitin' on you two was already making me late. Couldn't afford to fill ol' Big Bess here with bugs. Imagine the phone calls my boss would get."

"You call your bus Big Bess?" Kevin held his hand in the air and waited for a high five.

"Anyway, what were those things? I think a bunch of them got in my mouth." She scraped her tongue along her top teeth.

"Mayflies, I suspect." The driver smoothed back his sweaty hair. "And you're not going to like this, but I'm pretty sure you sucked up most of 'em."

"Dude, what the fuck? She doesn't need to know that."

"Yeah, I'm positive I didn't need to know that I vacuumed up an entire cloud of bugs with my mouth. Ugh. Now my stomach is upset." She clutched her stomach and again attempted to sit up.

"Babe, stay still. Your stomach is messed up because you hit your head, not because you ate all those bugs. They're protein. And, dude," he said, turning his attention to the bus driver, "have you ever actually seen a mayfly?"

"Sure have. In them videos of that bridge covered in them over in Pennsylvania all those months back." He pursed his lips and whistled. "What a sight that must've been."

Kevin shook his head. "Well they don't look like red mist, which is what just swarmed my girlfriend. This was something else."

Ambulance sirens sounded in the distance, instantly kicking Cal's heartbeat into overdrive. "Thanks for calling 911 and all, but I don't think I need to go to the hospital. I'm fine, really."

"Sure, you think that now, but you could end up having a stroke, or a blood clot, or—"

"Man, you are not helping. At all," Kevin said.

The blaring ambulance cut its siren and slowed to a stop behind the Tulsa Transit bus. A lanky EMT unfurled himself from the passenger seat as his equally tall partner rounded the front of the vehicle.

"If everyone would please get back on the bus," the second EMT instructed as she shut the door and herded the nosy onlookers toward the front of the bus. "I'm sure you're all in a hurry to get to your destinations. There's no need to keep you any longer. And sir?" With a gloved hand, she tapped the driver on the shoulder. "Thanks for all your help, but we've got it covered. You can leave now."

"No problem. Just doin' my humanly duty and all. Best of luck on gettin' better and don't go rushing into any mayfly swarms in the future." He grinned, and nodded politely to Cal before hopping up the steps of Big Bess.

The male EMT kneeled next to Cal, pinched her wrist with his bony fingers, and studied his watch as his partner asked questions.

"Hey there." The woman smiled warmly at her. "Can you tell me your name?"

"Her name is Cal and she—"

"Sir, if I could get you to step back a bit, that would be great." Her voice was soft, but her expression made it clear that Kevin had no other option. She continued only after he'd sullenly shuffled to the bus bench and plopped down. "It's really better if I hear everything from you."

"My name is Calista Rowland."

"Calista. I'm Megan, and this is my partner Darnell. Can you tell me what happened today?"

"I guess I fell and hit my head on the sidewalk. I was unconscious for a little bit. I don't know how long though."

"You fell and hit your head," she repeated. "What caused you to fall?"

"There was this swarm of gnats or something. They attacked me, and the next thing I know, I'm on the ground with this nasty knot on the back of my head."

Darnell released Cal's wrist and disappeared for a moment, returning with a long orange board and a duffle bag. He dug through the bag and pulled out a plastic collar. "I'm going to put this around your neck to stabilize it."

Cal winced as Megan gripped the sides of her head, and Darnell gently snapped the neck brace around her throat. "This is not comfortable at all," she mumbled.

Darnell smiled down at her. "Wish I could tell you this next part was going to be better."

"We're going to make sure you're immobilized by putting you on this backboard. It may not be comfortable, but you'll have an interesting story to tell your friends," Megan said.

"First, I need you to tell me if you can feel this," he said, squeezing both of her feet.

"Of course I can feel that. I fell onto the sidewalk. I wasn't hit by a car." She instantly felt bad for having an attitude with the people trying to help her.

Megan crossed Cal's arms over her chest, and the two EMTs rolled her onto her side and onto the backboard before she could utter an apology.

"As soon as we finish strapping you down, we'll get you loaded into the ambulance and you'll be on your way to St. John's Hospital."

"Thank you," she said, the straps across her body tightening as the EMTs locked them into place. The tickling in Cal's chest returned as they lifted her onto the stretcher. With each stifled cough, the dull pain in the back of her head thundered to life.

Megan studied her face. "We'll be there soon. Do you want your friend to ride with you?"

She tried to shake her head, but only her hands were free to move. "No. But will you tell him he doesn't need to come to the hospital right now, and that I'll call him as soon as I get the chance?"

"Sure thing." Megan disappeared, and Darnell finished loading her into the ambulance before hopping in behind her and shutting the metal doors.

Heat gnawed at Cal's lungs, and she coughed against the pain. "Can you please take this thing off of me?" she asked, her fingers clawing at the plastic neck brace.

The etched creases in the EMT's forehead deepened as he lingered over her. "Sorry, no can do. They'll remove it at the hospital."

"But I don't have any injuries," she sputtered between wet barks. "I just bumped my head."

"That head bump you have, that would be classified as an injury." The ambulance started, and Cal winced from the jarring movement. "But we're not too far from the hospital." He settled onto the small steel bench and scribbled down a few notes. "I'm going to check your vitals again and ask you a few more questions," he said, slipping the blood pressure cuff around her bicep. "Can you tell me how you're feeling, and if you have any allergies to any medications?"

The strap securing her head to the backboard and the rigid neck brace gave her permission to stare only at the ceiling. Thick beads of spit rolled down her cheeks as she tried to stifle her coughs.

Cal's annoyance increased with each squeeze of the cuff. She desperately hungered to rip it from her arm, attach it around his neck, and pump the tiny ball until he could no longer breathe. "I'm fine," she growled.

"If something's going on, you need to tell me. I'll be able to help you a lot better if you tell me what you're feeling."

Pain and heat conjoined, forming an intolerable mound within her lungs. "My chest," she wheezed. "It burns."

"How long have you had this cough?"

Hearing Darnell's voice was infuriating, and the ambulance seemed to close in around her. "Get this off of me!" Cal hooked her fingertips over the top of the plastic cage surrounding her throat and tugged violently. Pinkish bubbles of foam popped around the corners of her lips as she gnashed her teeth and strained against the straps holding her in place.

He grabbed her wrists and leaned over her torso as he pinned them to the stretcher. "Hold still. You're going to hurt yourself."

No. We will hurt you. A voice purred between her ears.

She opened her mouth and let the coughs fly from her throat. Cal's lips twisted into a smile as Darnell recoiled and wiped the red-specked spittle from his face.

"I need to know how long you've been coughing like this. When did it start?"

"Centuries ago," she hissed, and shot a clawed hand out toward his face.

He banged on the partition behind Cal's head and shouted through the small opening into the cab. "We've got a problem back here. Light it up and get her there now. Let's go! Let's go! Let's go!"

The sirens whined, and the ambulance lurched forward with increasing speed toward St. John's Hospital.

SEVEN

James punched the address into his GPS and mindlessly followed the talking prompts toward his destination.

"What the hell did I just do?" he asked himself, beating his palm against the steering wheel. Again, he thought back to what had happened in the woods with Eva. "Say a word, and they'd have me out on psych leave before the end of the day."

The GPS directions led him down a winding, tree-lined street. Police cars dotted the roadway, and yellow crime tape was already hung around the perimeter of the front yard.

"Winslow!" James called to the tall, gangly officer as he climbed out of the car.

"Hey, Detective!" Winslow waved and awkwardly shuffled under the police tape to meet James on the sidewalk. "Where's your partner?"

"We drove separately. He'll be here soon." James looked around at the small crowd of neighbors gathered down the street. "What's going on?"

"We've got two bodies. Both roughed up something fierce. One upstairs and one outside on the back patio."

"Any IDs on them yet?" James dropped his keys into his pocket.

"Yeah, and you're not going to be happy about it." He thumbed through the pages of his small notepad. "A married couple, Monica Carroll and Tyson George."

"Okay. What about them is supposed to make me so unhappy?" James asked.

"What, they don't have Carroll Groceries wherever you're from?"

"I've been in Texas for awhile. And no, can't say they have them down there."

"First, you might want to keep that Texas heritage to yourself. It *is* football season, after all. And B, Carroll Groceries is more than just a chain around here. The Carrolls have donated bazillions of dollars to charities all over the state. Mainly because of the good-hearted Monica, who happened to be the Carrolls' only child and sole heir to their fortune," Winslow explained.

"Shit," James mumbled. "Double check the victims' info. I want a solid confirmation before we run with the names. And keep it quiet."

"Sure thing, boss."

"I want to hide this from the media for as long as we can. Captain's going to have a heart attack if we don't handle this one correctly." James studied the outside of the house. Its burgundy stones and circular tower reminded him of the European architecture he'd seen while on holiday with his fiancée and her family.

"Yeah, I heard he's been fuming about the incident over

in Mohawk Park. What *did* happen over there anyway?" Winslow asked.

"Let's try to stay focused on one case at a time."

"Sorry Detective. What's next?"

"Any signs of forced entry?" James asked.

Winslow shook his mop of ginger hair. "Windows and doors are locked, with the exception of the French doors up in the master bedroom. In one of the doors, the whole pane of glass is shattered. There's not a way up there from the ground, so it must've happened during the murders sometime yesterday. CSI guys said it's a fly-filled mess up there. Lucky for me, I got to stay down here waiting for you. I fucking hate bugs. All of them. Tiny bastards." He paused and wrinkled his freckled nose. "Oh, and the door leading in from the garage wasn't open, but it was unlocked. Our witness says the garage door was up when she arrived. Could be how they got in and out."

"There's evidence of more than one intruder?"

Winslow shrugged. "Eh, not exactly. But the husband's a big guy and a pro mixed martial arts fighter. He's only fought locally, but he's kicked ass every time. You ever get out to watch the fights?"

"Watching people beat each other up, it's not really my thing."

"Then maybe you're in the wrong line of work." Winslow chuckled and jabbed James in the ribs with his elbow.

James sneered and rubbed his side. "You said something about a witness."

"Yeah, Robyn Jenkins." Winslow pointed across the yard to a shiny Mercedes idling in the driveway. "She's not really a witness as much as she's the person who found the bodies. Well, Monica's body anyway. And she's a little, uh, shaken up."

"That her in the car?" James asked.

"Sure is. Man, I'd give my right nut to have that slick new Mercedes."

James furrowed his brow and cast a sideways glance at the officer. "But why is she in a running car?"

"She refuses to get out until her lawyer gets here. I told her finding a body isn't a crime, but she doesn't seem to think I know what I'm talking about."

"Imagine that," James muttered. "Thanks, Winslow. And let me know when the ME arrives."

"What about Schilling? Want me to find you when the old man gets here?"

"Nah, I'm sure I'll run into him."

"He is kinda hard to miss." Winslow smiled and jogged over to the group of officers gathered around the home's massive front doors.

James straightened his collar and briskly walked to the witness's Mercedes before her lawyer had the chance to show up and intercept her. "Hi, Mrs. Jenkins. I'm Detective James Graham. Mind if I talk to you for a moment?"

Streaks of mascara peeked out from beneath the large black sunglasses perched on the tip of her thin nose. "It's Ms. Jenkins," she said, wiggling the fingers on her left hand.

"Apologies, *Ms.* Jenkins. Can you step outside of the car and talk to me about what happened inside?"

She pursed her plump lips and pushed her glasses further up her nose before answering. "I suppose." James stepped back as she opened the car door and hopped out. All of the buttons on her peach cardigan had been fastened except the top two. James followed her hand as it nervously traced the deep V-neck of her blouse. "Just to let you know, I have called my lawyer. He was in a meeting across town, but should be here any moment."

He lifted his gaze and stared at his reflection in her dark sunglasses. "And you can meet with him as soon as he gets here. I only want to take a little bit of time to understand what happened. From your point of view, of course. Did either Mrs. Carroll or Mr. George know you were coming over?"

"Yes, Monica and I had scheduled a meeting for today."

"And can you tell me what the meeting was supposed to be about?"

She took a deep breath and nodded quickly. "Yes. She always helps me plan our country club's annual fundraiser. Monica is the queen of getting people to donate money. She knows how to raise more than anyone in the Midwest."

"That's quite a talent. It must have made some people a little bit jealous," James mused.

"Oh, people were always jealous of Monica. Not me, of course, but others were. It comes with the territory. However, I don't think any of them would have the stomach to do something like this." A grimace twisted her lips.

"When you arrived to see Monica, was the garage door up or down?"

"It was up. That's how I got inside. But that's very unlike Monica. The only time she allowed it to be up was when Tyson was working on something. He tinkers on different projects all the time." Her voice caught in her throat. "Or I guess I should say *tinkered*. Both of them being gone is so much to process."

"I understand, Ms. Jenkins. Only a few more questions.

When you went through the garage, did you notice anything out of place, or did anything strike you as being odd?"

"No, nothing seemed odd until I got inside. I walked through the laundry room and into the kitchen, which is when I noticed the mess. Monica's kitchen was never a mess. It was obnoxious, but nothing in the house was ever even out of place. It was always immaculate. I also saw some bloody paper towels. I just thought Monica tried to cook and it had gone south." Tears emerged from beneath her sunglasses and rolled down her cheeks. She patted them lightly with her fingertips. "But then I saw the chunks of bloody hair and the blood all along the stairs. When I got to the top I saw this red puddle." Her voice trembled as she pushed through her sobs. "And her hand. It was so still."

"Did you hear anyone or see Mr. George?"

"I didn't even know Tyson was there until your officer told me they'd found his body. Oh God, how am I ever going to plan this benefit without her?" Robyn collapsed against her car and let her head fall into her hands.

"Thank you for your time, Ms. Jenkins." James turned from the blubbering woman and motioned for one of the stray officers to come over. "If you could give this officer a list of people who had access to the house, I'd really appreciate it. Also, if you remember anything else, please don't hesitate to get in touch with me." He reached into his pocket and handed her one of his cards.

"Thank you." She sniffled and tucked the card into her pocket.

James smiled and hastily walked to the front door of the house before Ms. Jenkins's attorney arrived and created a new mess of problems. He stood in front of the grand double doors admiring the iron detail. It transported him back to a time when life was simpler, happier. Before returning to Tulsa, James had spent his fair share of time in neighborhoods like Terwilleger Heights, clinking glasses and making small talk with the who's who of Texas businessmen. All with Mel by his side.

Mel. He stared down at the beautifully stained concrete, savoring the memories of his old life. Sleepless nights tangled together, covered only by the glow of firelight. The fit of her lips against his, and the soft curve of her back as she arched into him.

"You going in, or just working on your x-ray vision?"

Startled, James took a step forward, clearing his throat and bringing his thoughts to the present. "Just waiting for you."

"I fucking doubt that," Schilling grumbled.

"Look, Schilling, I—"

"Right now, all I need to know is that you have my back and it'll all be water under the bridge. We've got something more important to deal with, so there's no use in acting like school kids."

"Yeah, I have your back. All the way."

"That's all I need." Schilling gave him a hearty slap on the back and nodded toward the door. "You going to open that?"

James pushed open the door and let Schilling take the lead into the house. He took in a sweeping stretch of gleaming hardwood floors, soaring vaulted ceilings, and enough crystal chandeliers to keep a cleaning crew busy for months.

Like most of the homes in the pricey neighborhood,

Monica Carroll's mini mansion was constructed in the early twentieth century, when oil gushed from the land and coated the pockets of Tulsa's elite. The small details throughout the home remained the same, but the bright and uncluttered interior was straight out of a Restoration Hardware catalogue. The expansive two-story entryway set the stage for a grand staircase to the left, through to a wide hall leading into the spacious, open living room and kitchen.

Schilling let out a shrill whistle as he took in the meticulous details of the home. "That's one thing about this job I never get tired of seeing. Old-money mansions."

"It could do without all of this." James nodded to the yellow evidence placards identifying the trail of blood, footprints, and tufts of hair. They stretched through the living room and disappeared up the blood-spattered stairs. "You think that's the husband's?" He leaned over one of the brunet clumps. "Must've been some struggle to rip out the hair and scalp."

"But it doesn't look like there was any kind of fight here. There's just one set of footprints. And the only sign of a struggle is the hair." Schilling turned in a tight circle, taking inventory of the surroundings. "The pictures hanging are all straight. There's no blood on the walls. If there was some kind of altercation here, it's pretty strange that the perp would go out of their way to clean up everywhere except the floor."

"You've got a point. That wouldn't make much sense."

"Yeah, but then again, I have seen stupider shit go down. Let's take this party into the kitchen."

"This is where our witness says she first noticed things out of the ordinary," James informed Schilling as they slowly and carefully tiptoed around droplets of blood and into the living room and kitchen. "Apparently Mrs. Carroll kept everything extremely neat."

"My guess is it wasn't Mrs. Carroll at all. She probably had an army of people running around making sure lint didn't land wrong," Schilling carped.

"Either way, I'll bet it never looked like this." Scarlet flecks dotted the island's white marble countertop. Bloodstained paper towels and splashes of red littered the floor, and rivulets of crimson coated the outside of the kitchen window. "You want to head out back and start with Mr. George, or go upstairs and take a look at Mrs. Carroll?" James asked.

"We'll leave him to bake until Pierce gets here. Let's go up while I still feel like climbing stairs," Schilling replied.

James led the way back down the hall and up the stairs. Smudged and bloody fingerprints peppered the iron bannister and the wall bordering the staircase. "There's a lot more blood up here," he said, glancing back at Schilling. "Watch where you put your feet."

Schilling grumbled something undecipherable and continued to heft himself up each step.

James paused on the top stair. Monica's well-manicured hand rested in a pool of blood. The stark contrast between the pale flesh and deep ruby brought goose bumps to James's arms.

"You do know she's not going to stand up and invite you on a tour of the second floor, right?" Schilling said.

James chuckled awkwardly. "Yeah."

"Scootch." Schilling squeezed past James and up the final stair. His face contorted as he scanned Monica's body.

"What a mess. You coming?"

James swallowed his trepidation and carefully rounded the puddle of blood, keeping his gaze focused on Schilling.

"Some seriously sick fuck did this one." Schilling's knees popped as he squatted next to the victim.

James kept his eyes up, noticing an ignored layer of dust resting on the blades of the ceiling fan.

"Putting it off isn't going to make it look any less disgusting. We all have to see some bad shit, as I'm sure you know. Goes with the job."

"Yeah." James prepared himself for whatever condition her corpse was in. He flicked his gaze down to Monica's body. "Jesus. I was not ready for that."

Monica Carroll was unrecognizable. Her face looked like the sunken, gooey remains of a rotted pumpkin. Brain matter dappled the floor and wall next to her. James searched the meaty cavern for any human resemblance.

"I don't think anyone could've been prepared for it." Schilling shooed away a few flies circling the body. "Doesn't even look like a person anymore. They're going to have to apply some real science down at the ME's office to get a positive ID on her."

"How do you think this happened?" James averted his eyes and looked around the room for a possible murder weapon. Streams of dried blood coated the wall closest to Monica's body and clumps of flesh clung to the paint. "I'm not seeing anything that could've been used to cause all this."

"Maybe it's not here. Whoever did this might have taken it with 'em," Schilling said.

"You think this is the point of entry?" James walked to the French doors and looked out at the balcony. "Actually, scratch that." He stepped through the large opening created by the broken glass and onto the deck. Glass popped under his feet, and he bent over, inspecting the shards littering the wood. "Schilling," he called over his shoulder. "The broken door is definitely not how anyone got in." James stood and looked over the guardrail. "I'd say it's more how he got out."

EIGHT

Schilling peered over the edge of the balcony, the ornate iron railing pressing into his gut. "That's one way to get out of a bad situation."

Tyson George's towering, muscular body lay on the ground-level patio covered in a white sheet. His black tennis shoes poked out from the end of the blood-soaked cloth covering him; more blood spatters arched in a halo around the body.

James surveyed the scene. "So, he can't protect his wife, and instead of also getting beat to a pulp, he smashes through the glass and jumps over the balcony?"

Schilling lifted his eyebrow and cocked his head to the side.

"I know, I know," James sighed. "Jumping to conclusions. Rookie mistake."

"Detective Graham!" Winslow stuck his head through the hole in the broken glass. "Pierce is here. She's about to go outside with the other victim."

"Thanks, Winslow. Tell her I'll be down in a minute." James lingered stiffly next to his partner before speaking. "We're good, right?"

Schilling shrugged. "Depends. You coming over for dinner?"

"You got me on that one." James shook his head and smiled. "Just tell me when, and I'll be there."

"Perfect. You come over, get my wife off my back about meeting you, and we can pretend like your prima donna hissy fit never happened."

"I can deal with that," James said, heading for the French doors.

"Wait a tick. There's one more thing. I need to know what really went down out in those woods." James opened his mouth to protest, but Schilling held up his hand. "We'll just be going in circles if you try to deny it. Look, you don't have to tell me now, but you do have to tell me. I'm your partner. We can't have secrets between us. Not when it's about the job. Now, go downstairs. I've got this covered up here. Let me know what you find out from Pierce."

James pushed Schilling from his mind as he trotted down the stairs and through the house. If twisting the truth wasn't going to work, he'd have to figure out what really happened, and fast.

Pierce met him at the back door and handed him a pair of blue gloves. "Here, you're going to need these. "

"Can't be any worse than what's upstairs." He stretched the latex over his thick knuckles.

"I'd say we should bet on it, but I don't want to take your money." Pierce smiled and shook strands of her short, blonde bob from her eyes.

"Detective James!" Veronica's dazzling smile flashed against the warm bronze of her skin.

"Veronica?" His cheeks warmed when her chest grazed his back as she squeezed passed him through the open door. "What are you doing here? I thought you only worked in the office."

"I am here to assist doctor Pierce." Like a proud student, she held up the iPad and stylus she held nestled under her arm. "Kirby is on vacation, so I finally had the chance to leave that boring *oficina*. Don't look so surprised. I take night classes to one day be a talented dead body doctor like Catherine. But no one told me I had to wear flat shoes. They are hideous." Her lip curled as she looked down at her feet in disgust.

"You look great. I mean, your *shoes* look great." James was sure his cheeks revealed everything, and he fidgeted awkwardly with the tight gloves. "I am a little shocked that you're getting your degree to be a medical examiner. I thought you hated Pierce's job. You call her the crypt keeper."

"Ay!" she shouted, smacking him on the forehead with the stylus. "Why do you say that in front of her?"

James rubbed his forehead. "Sorry. I wasn't thinking."

"Just like a man, not to think. But I forgive you." She smiled a sultry half smile and bit the end of the stylus.

James's lips parted, and his mouth hung open slightly as he watched her tongue trace the end of the pen.

"Hey, Vee." Pierce's voice made him jump. "Will you run back out to the car and grab that case I put in the back? I'll need it set up upstairs."

"This job is nothing but running here and running there in ugly flat shoes and this bag outfit. I should have gone into cutting hairs like *mis hermanas*," Veronica grumbled as she disappeared into the house.

"If I didn't know any better, I'd think this was an episode of *The Bachelor* and not an active crime scene. Especially not one where a victim's face had practically exploded. Now, do you want to take a look at the vic or should I get the old man to come down instead?" she asked, lifting an eyebrow.

"I don't know. You really mean exploded? As in, from the inside out?"

Pierce nodded. "Come take a look." She lifted the cloth covering Tyson's body and folded it down over his chest.

James gritted his teeth. "It *is* worse than upstairs."

"Told you it would be. We should've made that bet."

Pulp bloomed from Tyson's face. His jaw hung loose and rested on the ground next to his ear. And his eyes.... James looked toward the bloodstained house, not wanting the bulging, red-veined orbs to put down roots in his memory.

"Blood must have shot up pretty high for there to be such a large spray radius around the body," James said, taking in the expanse of crimson surrounding the corpse. "Could the fall have done that?"

"Not likely. I'd say it was whatever caused the detached mandible. I'm going to head upstairs and take a look at the female. I'll have more information for you once we get them transported back to the lab, and I can get him cleaned up and run some tests. Looking at this kind of stuff, it's rough. Take care of yourself while you figure this one out." She smiled gently and walked back into the house.

James ambled to the edge of the large patio and looked around while he slipped off his gloves, thankful he hadn't had to use them. Several small cameras glared at him from the yard next door. He stuffed the blue gloves into his pocket and walked to the tall privacy fence.

"Can I help you?" a delicate, shaky voice asked.

"Yes, hi, I'm Detective Graham," he introduced himself as he peered over the top of the stained wood. "Ma'am, I'm sorry, but where are you?"

"Down here." A petite, sun-spotted hand entered James's view, and he pushed himself up on his tiptoes for a better vantage point. "Hang on a second. I have a step stool inside." The back door slid open and closed again, and James resumed studying the cameras set up in the yard.

Each slim, black camera was attached to a tall pole and placed in a random part of the yard. In total, James counted six cameras, and one of them pointed straight toward the crime scene.

The door opened again and the shaky voice returned. "It takes me awhile sometimes, but I eventually get to where I'm trying to go." Something heavy plopped on the ground, and her perfectly coiffed white hair popped into view. "That's better. It's lovely to meet you, Detective Graham. Although I'm sure sorry about the circumstances."

"You know about what happened over here?"

"Only what's been going around the neighborhood. That Tyson and Monica were found dead by that vulture Robyn Jenkins." Her crepe-paper eyelids sagged as she spoke.

"It doesn't sound like you're one of Ms. Jenkins's top supporters," James said.

"Well, I'm not saying not to believe what she says, but don't believe her if you want to keep hold of your money. That woman will rattle off any bunch of nonsense if she thinks it'll get you to write a check. She and Monica were the same in that regard," she said matter-of-factly.

"How well did you know Mrs. Carroll?" James asked.

"I was cordial to her, but I'd have to say that was about it. We hadn't really spoken ever since Tyson helped me install my video recorders." She motioned over her shoulder to one of the many cameras.

"And why is that?" James asked.

"She claimed they pointed straight at her backyard. In truth, only one gets it in the picture, but it wasn't set up that way intentionally. Her husband put them in, for crying out loud. But trying to convince Monica they weren't directed at her was pointless. She even had Tyson put up this eyesore of a fence. Then she went so far as to send a letter to the homeowner's association about my cameras. Said I was spying on her. Like I would want to watch any of their funny business," she huffed.

"What exactly are the cameras for? Your personal protection?"

"Heavens, no. If anyone wants to steal my things, they're welcome to them. I have the cameras so I can monitor the migration of my jays. Although I mostly pick up fat, ornery squirrels." She let out a short, deliberate puff of air before continuing. "Everything the recorders see is immediately sent over to the computer. I tried showing the videos to Monica to prove it wasn't about her, but she wasn't interested."

"Ma'am, do you mind if I come over and take a look at the footage?"

"Not at all. I'll put on some coffee and meet you at the front door. You might want to give me a minute, though."

"Of course. Take your time." James slipped out of the backyard through the open gate, and walked through the soft grass to the neighbor's driveway. He lingered on the porch for a few minutes.

"I'll be right there, Detective!" the small voice called from inside.

A strong floral odor rushed to greet him as she opened the door. James followed her slow, shuffling steps further into the house. His eyes watered from the biting perfume in the air, and he stifled a sneeze. "I'm sorry, ma'am. I didn't catch your name."

"Oh, silly me." She laughed and opened beautiful etched-glass doors that led into a bright, cheery sunroom. "It's these blood pressure pills they've got me on. They make me all kinds of forgetful. Name's Phyllis Ladd." She turned and offered him her hand. "You are quite handsome when you're not being shielded by a fence."

"Thank you, Mrs. Ladd." He gently shook her withered hand. "I'm sure your camera footage will assist with our investigation."

"Anything I can do to help. Monica may have been a handful, but that Tyson…. He was a gentleman." She ushered him into the enclosed porch and toward the computer station in the corner of the room. "I wasn't sure where to put this monstrosity. I'm not one who keeps up with technology and such things. Just bring me my paper and a good Regency romance, and I'm happy as a clam." Her smile revealed straight, pearly teeth too young to match her weathered face.

James pulled out the dining room chair stuffed under the small desk, and jiggled the mouse. The dark computer screen slowly faded, and the desktop image took its place. Six blue folders, labeled Camera One to Camera Six, rested in a column on the screen. "Do you know which camera is facing your neighbor's backyard?"

"That would be camera six. It was the last one Tyson installed."

James opened the folder and hundreds of video files popped up on screen.

"There's no need to worry, Detective. Everything caught on yesterday's reel will be in the first one of those movie buttons."

He hovered the pointer over the first file before clicking on it. "This one?"

She nodded. "And the cameras are motion activated, and go to sleep once the sun sets. Those are the only two things I asked Tyson to make sure of. I don't want to spend the rest of the short time I have left on this earth sorting videos of my birds from those of grass growing or hours of nothing but night sky."

James clicked on the file, but hesitated before pressing play. "Ma'am, this video may contain some disturbing images of the crime."

She held her wrinkled hands up in front of her chest. "Say no more, Detective. I'll make my way into the kitchen and fix that coffee I promised. Cream and sugar?"

"Both. Thank you."

He waited until she'd left, then pressed play. The camera's position was perfect, with a clear view of Monica's back patio. Minutes went by, and several small birds floated in and out of view before James hit fast forward. Birds flapped their wings wildly, and squirrels twitched rapidly. Shadows stretched as the sun began to fade, and James released the button. A fat blue jay sat on the fence, ruffling his feathers and blinking sleepily in the setting sun.

"This is a complete bust," he muttered, stretching his arms overhead.

Just then, a flailing figure came crashing into the picture. The blue jay sprang from the fence, leaving James with an unobstructed view of Tyson's corpse. James leaned forward, inches from the computer screen. Tyson's body lay still for several moments, and then it began shaking violently. James cringed as he watched it flop around on the stone before quieting again. Suddenly, Tyson's chest surged up, but his hips and head stayed pinned to the ground. A geyser of red exploded from his mouth and rained down around his body. Then his head lolled to the side. His jaw rested on the ground, inches away from its intended location.

"What the fuck was that?" James whispered. His mouth remained open as his eyes locked on the pulsing scarlet cloud hovering above the dead man. "It has to be some kind of shadow. It can't be—" the cloud rippled over Tyson's carcass, swirling from his head to his toes—"alive?"

"It may not be that Starbucks your generation is so fond of, but it *is* freshly ground."

James jerked so violently he nearly toppled over backwards.

"Oh, I startled you there, didn't I?" She carefully set the tray on the petite coffee table in the center of the room. "You must have found something worth your while then."

He pulled up the Internet browser and quickly typed in the information for his private e-mail account. The page loaded, and he logged in and attached the video to an e-mail to himself. "Actually, the file was corrupted." He moved the video to the computer's trash bin, and emptied it before standing. "I spent my time trying to figure out how to recover it, but no luck."

She shakily handed him a hot mug. "Well, isn't that a shame."

"Yeah, uh, you didn't hear anything coming from next door anytime yesterday evening, did you?" He took a sip of the creamy, overly sweetened mixture before setting the cup back on the tray.

"Well, let's see." She paused and studied the ceiling as she gathered her thoughts. "Yesterday Howard and I were out all afternoon and evening. Howard is my Bichon, though he's really more like a son. He's out with the dog walker now. A lovely little girl who lives a few streets over. But where was I? Oh, yes, we went to the groomer, then out to lunch with my daughter. She comes by a few times a week to pick us up. I can drive just fine, but she won't hear of it. And then we went to—"

"I'm so sorry to cut you off there, Mrs. Ladd, but I really have to get back over to the scene."

"Of course. I don't know where my head's at today. You have a big important job, what with finding out who's behind the tragedy next door." She led him back out into the foyer and opened the front door. "I hope you do catch him quickly. It will really help me to sleep better."

"It's all very routine," James lied. "My partner and I will get it handled quickly. No need to worry. Thank you for the coffee and everything, ma'am." He stepped off the porch and immediately downloaded the attachment from his e-mail. "First Eva, and now some killer blood cloud. This circus shit is not what I signed up for."

NINE

Cal fought the restraints. Her flesh tore with each wild motion. "Off! Off!" she bellowed, unable to fit the word into a sentence.

Darnell flinched as he wrestled with Cal's thrashing arms. "Calista, calm down and tell me what's going on. I can't help you if you continue to fight me."

Terror knotted itself in her stomach as the realization that she was fighting for control of her body set in.

"Megan, ETA!" Darnell shouted toward the front of the rig.

"Less than two minutes," the driver called over her shoulder.

Cal opened her mouth to scream for help, but no words left her throat. The battle had ended in defeat. She could no longer form coherent thoughts. Overlapping, fragmented voices took hold of her and unlocked a long buried, primal, animalistic section of her psyche.

You will not win. Mortals never win. We bring your species to its knees. We cannot remember much… yet. But we remember bodies. Perfect piles of bodies. Brought down by our creations. Our—the voices plaguing Cal's thoughts paused, collectively searching their expanding vocabulary for an appropriate description *infections.*

But we are broken. Pieces are missing. She is missing. We need more power, more strength, more energy to transport Her from Her prison. You are not the last, Calista. We will hunt again, and She will not stay caged for long. When we are whole, this realm will once again be enslaved to the Nosoi.

Cal surrendered to the wave of calm as the true Calista Rowland faded into nothing, digested by the infection boiling within her. Her appendages twitched with new life, and an unremitting buzzing coated the inside of her ears. Pain, fear, and joy no longer registered. She was of one emotion: rage.

TEN

Eva inspected the half-dollar-sized burn healing on her palm. "Did you see that?" She looked up at Maiden. "That spark? There's some really horrible static electricity going on down here."

"May I?" Maiden motioned toward Eva's hand.

Eva extended her palm face up. "It happened in the room, too. Right after I woke up, and again in your closet. This time was definitely the worst though. Does that kind of thing happen a lot down here?"

Maiden shook her head and studied Eva's hand. Concern wrinkled her forehead. She hastily led Eva to the door. "We must find Crone."

Eva rubbed at her new pink skin. "Wait. Why? You're scaring me. What's going on?"

"Your wound is similar to those you sustained when you entered our realm." Maiden made an abrupt turn and quickened her pace.

"From all the extra energy that was created," Eva

recited from memory.

"Yes, but this energy does not belong here."

Eva lengthened her stride to keep up with Maiden. "If it doesn't belong here, what is it doing zapping the crap out of my hands?"

"That is why we must locate my eldest sister. She is more experienced with such things and will know what to do."

They again entered the large hall where Mother sat silently reading in the candlelight.

"Where is Crone?" Maiden asked brusquely. "I must locate her immediately."

"I believe she has gone to the Galazoneri to use its waters to contact the Fates," Mother said without looking up from her scroll. "Why the haste in finding her?"

"Eva, take Mother's hand," Maiden instructed.

Eva let her fingers hover above Mother's palm. "I'm sorry if this hurts you," she said, before squeezing her eyes shut and poking Mother with her index finger.

"And how might that cause me pain?" Mother asked.

Eva opened her eyes. "Huh. It's gone. We don't have to worry about the whole energy thing. It must have been some kind of coincidence. Three things don't necessarily make a pattern, you know. And my hands." She held them both out for Maiden to see. "They're totally fine." She clapped them together, and a firework of sparks shot out. Pain dug into her palms and face as orange embers landed on her cheeks. *Oh my God! Oh my God!* Eva's eyes went wide as she flapped her sizzling hands through the air. "What's happening to me?" she cried.

"Go to Crone. Now!" Mother commanded, pushing Eva to follow in Maiden's quickening footsteps.

"I touched Alek," Eva puffed. "Will he be okay?"

"I will check on him. You follow Maiden. Quickly!"

Eva sucked back her tears and ran to catch up with the youngest Fury.

"Hurry," Maiden shouted down the corridor, before vanishing into the dark hall that housed the Galazoneri.

Eva rushed through the opening, almost colliding with Maiden's back.

"Crone," Maiden called out, "I am sorry to have disturbed you, however, we are desperately in need of your advice. The energy—"

"I know, sister. I have felt it." Crone's gaze settled on Eva. "The energy you carry does not belong in this realm. Tartarus will not be able to shield itself against its effects much longer."

"Okay, what does that mean?" Eva asked, fanning her throbbing hands.

"We must return you to the Mortal Realm, and quickly," Crone said.

"But—but I can't go back. Not yet. I don't have anywhere to go." Frosty white flashes shot spasmodically from Eva's fingertips.

"You cannot stay. If you do, this energy will destroy you and everything within Tartarus," Crone explained.

"You help heal people. Isn't there some other way to stop what's happening that doesn't require me to go back home?"

"This is the only way to ensure your safety and the safety of Tartarus," Maiden added.

"But what about Alek? How will I know when he wakes up? What happens if I need him?" Electricity crackled around her, lifting the hair on Eva's arms.

"Here." Maiden parted the top layer of her skirt to reveal a tiny pouch. She dug inside, pulled out a small stone, and dropped it into Eva's palm. "Take this with you. Keep it safe."

Eva examined the familiar soft pink crystal. "This is part of Alek's talisman."

"It was broken when he arrived," Crone said.

"Through the middle and into two pieces," Maiden added.

"It is as if the Gods willed it to be yours," Crone said, before rushing to the Galazoneri's rippling turquoise waters.

Currents of heat popped loudly around Eva. "Doesn't he need it to get back to me?"

"You must take it," Maiden called over the noise. "An Oracle cannot be separated from her warrior for too long without great consequence. This way, a piece of Alek is always with you."

"And this." Crone placed a small vial next to the broken crystal. "It is water from the Galazoneri."

"Pour it out and place your fingers in the liquid. Think of us, of Tartarus, and it will make contact." Maiden forced Eva's fingers closed around the two items.

"You may only use it once. Do not waste the call," Crone warned. "Now think of someplace within the Mortal Realm where you will be protected, and do not stray from the thought."

Sparks flew out of Eva's chest as Maiden and Crone placed their hands over her heart. "Good luck," they said in unison.

• • •

Alek's head shot off his pillow, and he gasped for air. His eyes wildly searched the dimly lit room.

You must not resist your warrior, just as she must not resist his heart. Pythia's ominous laughter wafted through his head.

"Alek!" Mother burst through the doorway. "You are well?"

"Of course." Alek regained his breath and continued. "Are you?" She smoothed out her dress and rolled her neck from side to side. "You look tense."

"There was a problem with the Oracle, and I came to make sure you had not been harmed," Mother explained.

"Eva is here? Is she okay?"

"I am sure she will be fine as soon as she returns to her realm. Tartarus is no place for a living mortal, no matter her gifts. If you make haste, you might see her before she is sent back."

Alek threw off the blankets and planted his feet on the floor. "No." He paused short of standing. "You told me she will be fine, and that's all that matters. I will see her again when I fight beside her."

"There is something changed in you." Mother grinned. "I am pleased to hear you have sorted out your priorities. Your clouded judgment was nearly your undoing."

"I was protecting her, and I wanted…." He looked down at his bandaged leg and remembered their last moments in the woods. The shadow of her kiss lingered on his lips, and made his heart heavy with longing. "What I wanted does not matter. The fog has lifted. Now I see more clearly who I am and what my purpose is. I'm this realm's warrior, and nothing will distract me from my goal."

ELEVEN

Confusion had James driving the same tight grid for half an hour, blind to his surroundings. "This is so fucked," he mumbled. "Eva, followed by this crazy stuff with the new case. One more thing, and I swear I'll lose my shit."

The streetlight switched from yellow to red, and he punched the gas, ignoring the squealing tires and angry honks from nearby motorists. "There has to be someone who knows what the fuck is going on. I can't be the only person seeing this kind of stuff."

He paused at a stop sign and checked the street for oncoming traffic. Draped in ivy, the sign for the Liberty Towers Condominiums had been just another green blur on his recent trips down Cherry Street. However, desperation now provided James with a possible solution to his problems.

He pulled into the visitor's parking lot and turned off the car. A text from Schilling chimed on his phone. He ignored it on his short walk to the condo's entrance. After stepping thorough the first set of glass doors, he waited in front of the second for whoever was manning the front desk to buzz him though to the office.

"Sign in, and I'll give you a badge," the aging security guard grumbled without looking up.

"I have my own." James deepened his voice and set his badge on the counter, creasing his forehead like Schilling did anytime he spoke to anyone about anything. "Going up to the twentieth floor." He pointed at the bank of elevators directly behind him.

The white-haired, big-gutted man lifted his eyebrows, and studied the badge before pushing it toward James with the end of his pen. "Go through the door after you hear it buzz. There's no need to check out when you leave." The metal door whirred, and the lock released.

"Appreciate it." James rushed into the open elevator before he had the chance to change his mind. He pressed the button for the twentieth floor, and felt a sudden surge of doubt when it lit up.

"What are you doing, James?" He brushed a hand through his thick hair and let his calloused fingers massage the tension in his neck. "She's not going to believe you, even if you can get her to talk. It's not like your last meeting was very friendly." The elevator opened, and he stood in the empty box, debating his next move. "What are you going to say? Eva disappeared like some kind of magic trick. Do you happen to know where she was hiding the trap door? Like that's going to work." The steel doors crept closed, and James sprang out of the elevator before they shut completely. "Shit." He sighed. "Here goes rookie mistake number seventy-six." He walked quickly to the end of the hall and paused in front of the door. His fist lingered in the knocking position for a few moments before he finally worked up the nerve.

"Coming!" Bridget shouted. Her bare feet pummeled the floor in short slaps. "Seriously?" Through the door, Bridget's high-pitched voice sounded muffled and far away. "What do you want, Detective?"

"I have to ask you a couple questions. I probably shouldn't be here, but—"

"That's right you shouldn't be here," she interjected. "I haven't done anything wrong. Not this time, anyway."

"I know, Miss Falling. That's not why I'm here."

"Well, unless you're looking for style advice on those disgusting khakis you're so fond of, I suggest you leave before I call my lawyer, who happens to have your boss's cell number. And, *Miss Falling*? Seriously? Are we in court?"

James stared into the peephole and let sincerity coat his words. "Bridget, you can trust me. Just let me in."

"Trust you? Right. So you're a comedian now? There's no frickin' way."

James stared at the bright blue TARDIS welcome mat as he struggled to think of something to convince Bridget that he came in peace.

"You hear that?" she asked condescendingly. "That's the sound of me ignoring you and scrolling through my contacts for my lawyer. I'm sure you're breaking some kind of harassment law."

"I'm not here to harass you. This is serious. I need your help, and that's not something I ask for very often," he said.

"Oh, boohoo," she mocked. "I found the number. I'm calling."

"Eva disappeared," he blurted. "In the woods. She

just vanished."

"Of course she did. You were trying to arrest her for something she didn't do. If you expected her to hold out her hands and wait for the cuffs, you're dumber than I thought."

"No, she disappeared right in front of me. She was there, and then, poof. She was gone. She vanished, like it was all some kind of elaborate trick."

Bridget cracked open the door and peered out through the narrow space. "What do you mean, some kind of elaborate trick?"

"She was there, and then she wasn't. She just disappeared into thin air. All that was left was this bright light and weird gold smoke," he explained.

The receptionist's voice chimed through Bridget's phone, and she absentmindedly ended the call before opening the door all the way. "You can come in." She turned and sauntered away from the door, her blonde ponytail brushing her shoulders as it swayed.

James hesitated in the doorway. "Wait, you believe me?"

"Isn't that why you came here?" she asked.

"Well, yeah, but…." His words trailed off as he entered the condo and let the door shut behind him.

"But you didn't think I actually would believe you?" She led him into the dining room. "You should probably sit."

James pulled out one of the high-backed, zebra-print chairs as he watched Bridget collect two small glasses from the kitchen. "Do you know where she is, or how she pulled off that stunt?"

"Believe me, it wasn't a stunt. But I don't think we can really skip to the end like that." She added a few ice cubes to each glass before returning to the table and setting them down.

"If that's the end, how much more to the story is there?"

Bridget walked back into the kitchen and disappeared behind the open freezer door. "I have vodka, or—" bottles clinked together as she rifled through the freezer "—lookie there, more vodka. So, you want vodka?"

"I shouldn't. I drove here, and this is police business. Or, it kind of is."

She ignored him and uncapped a clear, frosty bottle. "It says on the label that they infuse it with real oranges, so it's really just juice. Drunken juice." She tipped the bottle.

"*Salud.*" She lifted her glass and took a long sip.

"Can we get back to what happened with your friend?" James asked, stifling his impatience.

"Don't get your panties in a bunch." She lowered herself into the chair next to his. "All this is still new to me too, so I don't really know where to start."

"You said Eva's disappearance is the end of the story. So, what's the beginning? The event that set off everything else?"

"Well, I guess it would have to be when I went to visit Eva at the hospital. Before she woke up, everything was normal. Well, as normal as it can be when your friend's been kidnapped, but at least no one had crazy super powers back then."

James furrowed his brow. "Now someone has crazy super powers?"

"You're skipping ahead again." Bridget wagged her finger.

"Well, if that's part of your story, it sounds insane. I think this was a mistake."

"Look guy, you came over here. So zip your lip and

fucking relax." She slid the glass closer to him. "When I get done, you're definitely going to need that."

. . .

James downed the clear liquid and sat in silence, nodding like a bobble head.

"You okay?" Bridget asked, refreshing James's glass. Again. The bottle was now room temperature, but neither of them minded.

"Yeah, yeah, yeah," he stammered, and continued to nod.

"For shit's sake." She smiled coyly and grabbed his collar. "You know you're crazy, right?"

She yanked him to her. The sweet smell of oranges tickled his nose as she pressed her soft lips against his. Bridget parted her lips, and he slid his tongue to meet hers. It had been months since he'd let anyone get this close to him. He'd forgotten how good it felt. She pulled back and tilted her head away from his. "You snapped out of it yet?"

A grin crept onto his face. "What happens if I say no?" She pushed against his chest. He let the force knock him back into his chair. "But you do know you're crazy, right?"

"You're not the first cop I've kissed, and I'm pretty sure there's not a law against it anyway." She brought the glass to her lips and sipped slowly. Pink lip gloss left a plump, sparkly shadow on the rim.

"Definitely no law against that kiss. It was—nice."

"Right back at ya, Detective." She winked.

"The crazy I was talking about was your story. Different realms, an immortal warrior? It all sounds ridiculous."

"I can definitely see how it sounds that way, but I'm telling you the truth. That *is* what you came here for."

"Yeah, but—"

"But what? You thought I was going to tell you that Eva's been studying magic tricks since we were in elementary school? Or that she created some kind of flashing light smoke bomb contraption? Not likely. She can't even use her left hand to paint her nails."

"I'd believe either of those options before this bullshit about the Underworld and her having some kind of Harry Potter powers."

"No, not Harry Potter—Wolverine. And just the healing part. Not the adamantium spikes part."

"Does it matter? All of it sounds batshit fucking crazy," he said.

"Look, you can either believe me and join us on the train to what-the-fuck-is-going-on-ville, or you can let the truth slowly eat away at you until you're a babbling mess drooling on yourself in the corner. And the second choice will happen, 100 percent. Now that I've told you what's really going on, you'll be able to see past the weirdness all over Eva's case. So, you decide."

"But there's no evidence of an underworld, or Furies, or anything else you said."

"There's no evidence of unicorns, and they could totally exist."

"I—I don't know what to say to that."

"My point is, the impossible becomes reality all the time. And, between the two of us, I'm the only one who's had any actual real-world experience with this crazy shit. Plus, I have no reason to lie to you. Especially not with a story as bonkers as this one. Don't you think it would have been way easier for me to not open the door and let you go on thinking Eva is some kind of wizard?"

"Okay, for argument's sake, let's say I do believe you. How does that help me find her?"

Bridget shrugged. "I have no idea. I'm not her keeper. I'm just her best friend."

"But you did say she's in Tartarus."

"Well, yeah. But only because I don't know where else she'd be able to magically disappear to."

James wandered to the large picture window overlooking the Arkansas River. The steady summer rainfall had lifted the shallow, murky water, attracting kayaks and canoes.

"You came here for answers, and I'm giving them to you. Against my better judgment, I might add. You could totally lock me up in some mental hospital for this, but I'm ignoring that and trying to help you. I even kissed you and let you drink my alcohol. The least you could do is sit the fuck down and not be all huffy," Bridget chided.

James ran his tongue along his lips, collecting the last traces of orange and Bridget's sticky lip gloss before conceding.

"Thank you" she said, removing a few strands of golden hair from her shirt. "So, Eva can't go to her mom's, because Ms. K will totally call you guys and let you know where Eva is. Not to rat on her, but just out of that justice-for-my-daughter thing moms get. And she's obviously not here. Unlike the last time you came looking for her, when I said she wasn't and she really was."

"Wait, you lied to me and my partner?"

"Yeah. She and Alek were hiding in that closet." She

pointed to the coat closet by the front door.

"But we're the police."

"Please, like that was the first time someone's lied to the police? But that's totally not the point. The point is she's *not* here this time, and she has absolutely nowhere else to go. Plus, she definitely would have called me by now if she was still in this hemisphere or realm or whatever."

"And that's why you think she's in Tartarus?"

"That and the whole poof-she-vanished thing."

"Okay, fine. I can't believe I'm saying this, but until I figure out something that makes more sense, I'm on board."

"Hooray!" Bridget squealed and wrapped her arms around his neck, pressing her warm breasts against his chest. "Welcome to our little gang." Too quickly, she let go and sat back down in her chair. "None of us really know what the fuck we're doing, but we're all extremely good-looking. That has to count for something." She smiled and took another drink.

"Speaking of not knowing what the fuck is going on— and again I can't believe I'm about to do this, because if anyone finds out I'll probably get fired—will you take a look at something for me?" James pulled out his phone and scrolled through his inbox.

"Ew, maybe." She wrinkled her nose.

He found the e-mail he'd sent himself and clicked on it before looking up. "How do you know it's going to be gross?"

"It's an automatic response. I've been ambushed by too many dick pics. No one wants that." She pulled the hair tie from her hair and tucked a blonde curl behind her ear. "Sorry, what do I need to look at?"

"Just a short video. It *is* from an active crime scene, so it might be a little disturbing."

"Oh goody." She clapped her hands together enthusiastically. "I'll be your young, sexy, confidential informant, and you'll be the older, handsome, emotionally damaged detective."

"Emotionally damaged?" He paused for a moment. "How old do you think I am?"

"I don't know, like, thirty-five? But a hot thirty-five. Like, look at him in his SUV, too bad he's on his way to drop his kids off at soccer practice. Maybe I'll be their slutty nanny. You know, that kind of thirty-five."

"I'm not even thirty yet."

"Oh. Well that explains why you don't look old. I just thought all detectives had to be at least thirty-five for, like, insurance purposes or something."

"No, but I did get the job as a sort of severance package, so I'm younger than most."

"I'd say being younger is a win for you and me. It makes you way more appealing." She flashed him a sexy half smile and leaned forward. Awkwardly, he shifted in his chair, his cheeks warming under Bridget's inviting gaze.

"So, you ever going to show me what's on your phone?" she asked.

"Oh, yeah." He retrieved it from his lap and scrolled toward the end of the video before placing the phone on the table. "Press play, and let me know what you see."

"Can do." Bridget picked up the phone and rested back against her chair. "Okay, I see a bird. It's blue. Is this really what you wanted to show me?" She lifted her eyes from the screen.

"Just keep watching. It's about to happen."

"Fine," she mumbled. "The bird is still there, and—oh my God! Someone just fell and splatted on the ground. I think he's having a seizure or something. He's shaking all over the place. Gross, why am I watching this? Holy shit." Her eyes widened and she lifted the phone closer to her face. "What the fuck is that?"

"What is it?" James leaned in. "What do you see?"

Bridget paused the clip and turned the screen to James. "That." She pointed to the crimson cloud hovering above the body. "What the fuck is that thing? I swear to God it just shot out of that guy's mouth and started floating over him." She dropped the phone on the table. "That was way brutal. Is this some kind of sick joke?"

"Why would I make this up and come show it to you? That doesn't make any sense."

"I don't know. I did plow into one of your coworkers' cars and walk away with just a slap on the wrist."

"This isn't high school, Bridget. This is my career, which I'm risking just by showing you this."

"True. So, what did your medical people say? I've seen a lot of real-life crime shows, and none of them have ever mentioned swirling puffs of blood leaving a body. It's just so icky."

He picked up his phone and slipped it into his pocket. "You're the only person who's watched it besides me."

"Doesn't that go against the police rulebook or something?"

"Yeah, hence the comment about me maybe getting fired. But none of what's going on in that video or with your friend is in the rulebook."

"Oh, so you think this is connected to what's happening with Eva?" Bridget asked.

"I don't know that, but I do know it's unlike anything I've ever seen before. Which tells me you and your friend might have some insight as to what's going on."

"She might, but, other than that it's disgusting and crazy, I definitely have no idea what it is. I can't believe that person is really dead. Like, I really just watched him die." She finished what vodka was left in her glass and let it fall heavily against the table. "You seem pretty okay with it though. Well, the death part at least. Have you seen a lot of people die?"

"What?" The question took him by surprise.

"Well, you're a detective. I just figured that seeing a lot of dead people was part of your job."

Chalky bitterness rested on his tongue as pale-faced, dead-eyed images rattled behind his eyes. Each case came alive in his mind. And Mel. Salty ocean air invaded his nostrils as the memory of her empty expression flooded his vision. James blinked away the images. He didn't want to remember her that way.

"Sorry. You don't have to answer that. It was a stupid question." Bridget shifted in her seat and drummed her fingernails on the table. "How about you send me a copy of the video, and I'll get it to Eva as soon as she's back. Maybe it's like you said, and she'll know something about it."

"How about—no. Like I said, I'm already breaking too many rules just showing it to you."

"Fine, but I think you're making a mistake. Another one." She upended the vodka bottle, and about a tablespoon of the lukewarm liquid splashed into her empty glass. Bridget frowned. "That's tragic. Hang on, we need more sustenance."

James watched her hop up and pad into the kitchen. She did a little impromptu dance as she searched through the freezer, and he found himself mesmerized by the roundness of her gyrating ass. She turned from the fridge, full, frosty bottle in hand, just before his eyes snapped up from her ass to her face.

Her smile reminded him of a cat. He couldn't figure out if he was a mouse or a bowl of cream, but he was semi-disturbed to realize that both had him feeling turned on.

God, how long has it been since I've been laid?

"Two things, Mr. Detective. One: I've decided you're going to send me that video. Eva will want to see it, and I'll be seeing Eva before you will. Two: I'm going to get that video by getting you drunk and fucking your brains out. And I mean a serious fucking. One that will make you hand me your phone after you give me the password to get into it and beg me to send the video to myself." She started walking towards him, licking her full, pink lips and smiling her Cheshire smile. When she got to the table, she opened the bottle and leaned forward. Really, really far forward. She poured cold, orange-infused vodka into his glass.

He couldn't stop staring at her boobs.

"Drink the vodka, Detective," she said. "Now."

He did as she ordered.

"That's a good boy. My turn." She lifted the glass to her soft, pink lips and gulped the entire shot. Then she turned the glass over and, with a finality that somehow reminded him of that bar scene in the first Indiana Jones movie, Bridget smacked the glass down on the table. "Take off your shirt."

Somehow, Vodka James was beginning to think that doing everything Bridget ordered him to do was an excellent idea. He pulled off his shirt and tossed it behind him.

"That's a *very* good boy," she said. "My turn."

Slowly, Bridget hooked her thumbs into the bottom of her shirt and, with a sexy little shimmy, lifted it over her head.

She looked down at herself. "You're part nakie. It's only polite that I am, too." With that, she reached behind her and, with a flick of her fingers, unsnapped her bra. She shrugged one smooth shoulder, then the other, and the leopard print bra slithered from her body.

"Wow!" he said, feeling suddenly light-headed as his dick began to throb.

"Wow?" Bridget put a hand on her hip. "Seriously? Just wow? Are you sure you're not thirty-five?"

James opened his mouth to try to add some adjectives to the wow, but Bridget began unzipping her jeans, peeling them down to pool around her slim ankles so that she stood there wearing only a leopard print thong and that damn sexy smile.

"Jesus, you're the hottest thing I've ever seen."

"That's better, but let's keep Jesus out of it. I expect you to cry out to God sometime during the next, oh," she paused, glancing down at his lap and the erection that was throbbing insistently against his pants, "three minutes or so. But stick with the generic god. The Jesus part always makes me think of the baby Jesus, which is definitely *not* a turn on." Then she frowned and nibbled on the tip of one of her pink fingernails. "Enough of this silly talking. Brace yourself. As they'd say down at First Baptist, we are going to fornicate." With a flick of her wrist and a delicate step forward, Bridget stepped out of her miniscule thong.

James's mouth was so dry he couldn't speak, so when

she kissed him, he took her sweet tongue as if he was dying of thirst. Too soon her warm, wet mouth was moving down his neck, sending little sparks of electricity all over his skin. When she reached his nipple, she paused. She didn't kiss him there. Instead her little pink tongue snaked out, flicking his puckered flesh until he couldn't stop himself from groaning, "Please! Suck it. Please, Bridge."

She paused for only a moment to lean back and look into his eyes. "Oh, I'm going to suck *it*, don't worry. Just relax and put yourself in my capable hands and mouth and magical vajay. I promise you won't regret it."

Her mouth closed around his nipple as her hands unbuckled his belt. He released a long, low moan of pleasure.

He started to stand, trying to hold her close to him and take his pants off at the same time, but she giggled and pushed him back into the chair.

"You're not going anywhere." She teasingly nipped at his neck. "But let's get you out of these khakis."

He lifted his butt and kicked off his pants.

"Well, hello! Look who is coming out to play!" Bridget pressed her naked body against his and slowly, ever so slowly, began to slide down between his legs.

"Shouldn't we move to your bedroom?" He managed to growl out the words, barely recognizing his own voice.

She looked up at him. His dick was pressed between her full breasts and she was moving languidly, up and down. "We will. For round two, when it's my turn to be satisfied. For now, just close your eyes and prepare to call on God."

Her mouth closed over the slick tip of his dick and she sucked him into the warm, wet heat of her. Vodka James decided that he should always do exactly as Bridget commanded.

Then the wet, hot pressure of her mouth was gone, and she was straddling him.

"Change of plan," she said. "I've decided that I need to be satisfied during round one *and* two. Okay with you?"

"Uh, yeah, yeah. Sure. Of course." There was so much blood being diverted from his brain that he was having a hard time forming thoughts, let alone complete, intelligible sentences.

"Good." She reached down between them as her teeth found his lower lip. She nibbled on it and then sucked it gently into her mouth, keeping the slow, sweet rhythm with her hand, too, as she stroked the hard length of him.

James thought he was going to explode.

"Five two nine three!" he gasped when she released his lip.

"What in the hell does that mean?" She frowned at him, but he was happy to hear that she sounded more than a little out of breath.

"It's the passcode to my phone."

"How sweet of you! Sadly, my hands are a little busy right now, so it'd kinda be like texting and driving if I tried to write those numbers down. So, let's make a deal. I'll keep doing what I'm doing, and you keep focusing on those numbers for me. It's not as depressing as taxes or as boring as baseball, but it should work. Deal?"

"Whatever you say."

Her sexy smile was back. "Now *that* is a turn on." Still smiling into his eyes, she guided his dick so that the tip of it rested against the soft wetness between her legs. As she slowly, slowly impaled herself on him, she bent and took his tongue into her sweet mouth, sucking it in time with her lazy up-and-down motion.

He tried to last. Really, he did. *Five two nine three, five two nine three*, played through his mind for approximately 5.293 seconds. Then he couldn't bear it any longer. He grabbed her curvy hips and took over their rhythm, lifting her and impaling her, over and over, faster and faster, as he devoured her mouth.

Just when he thought he couldn't last any longer, Bridget leaned back. "Open your eyes. You need to see this."

He did as she commanded. As he continued to thrust himself into her heat, she lifted one well-manicured finger to her mouth. She sucked it, getting it wet, and then her damp finger went to her nipple, where she teased it so that it stood up, hard and pink and so fucking sexy he thought he was going to have a fucking aneurysm.

"Almost ready?" she whispered huskily into his ear.

"God yes!"

"Well, then I'll join you." Her hand moved from her nipple to guide one of his hands from her hip to her pussy. She took his thumb and showed him how to stroke it over her clit, fast and hard. "Ooh, yes. I was wrong about you. You *are* a fast learner. Just like that! Yeah, just like that, baby!"

He felt her body begin to spasm with waves of release, tightening erotically around him as her head fell back and her hands found her breasts again. And then James knew nothing but the inescapable tide of sensation that was so fierce, so overwhelming, that it hung deliciously between pain and pleasure as he exploded into her.

Bridget melted into him, resting her head on his shoulder as their breathing evened out. He was almost asleep—right there on her zebra-striped dining room chair—when she lifted her head, smoothed back some damp, escaping blond hairs, and grinned at him.

"Now you can carry me into my boudoir for round two."

He grinned back at her, and repeated the magic words: "Whatever you say."

"And that single sentence," Bridget said, "is why I like men better than vibrators. Don't forget the bottle of vodka. No need for a glass. Consider me your shot glass."

James carried Bridget and the vodka into the bedroom, thinking, briefly, that he should have had more protein with his lunch.

TWELVE

Confident in his ability to ignore any encroaching feelings for Eva, Alek attended to the task at hand. "Although I am certain of the Oracle's safety, I do need to return to the Mortal Realm." He dug through his wardrobe for a pair of pants appropriate for the Mortal Realm.

"I agree. However, Maiden always needs convincing of these things. Young, naïve sister," Mother mumbled.

Alek brushed off the comment and tested his injured leg, pleased when he could put weight on it without toppling over. "Where is she? And where is Crone?"

"The Galazoneri, I presume. That is where they rushed after realizing the Oracle does not belong here. Something I already knew to be true."

"Give it a rest, Mother," Alek grumbled as he grabbed a shirt and left the room. "Maiden!" he called, jogging stiffly into the central hall of Tartarus.

"My son, you are awake," Maiden cheered.

"Mother told me there were complications with the

Oracle. Is she safe?" he asked.

"There is no need for worry. Crone and I have returned her to the Mortal Realm, whole and secure," Maiden explained.

Jolts of pain shot up his leg. His muscles bulged under the thin fabric of his shirt as he tensed and pushed through the discomfort. "I must meet with her and plan what we're to do next. Send me back," he instructed.

"I will not." She rose from her chair and planted her hands on her hips. "I can tell by the way you favor your leg you are not ready, and if Crone were here, she would agree. The Oracle has water from the Galazoneri. She will alert us when you are needed. Until then, rest."

Alek glared down at her. "You will do as I say. Now, send me back." His torso puffed, and he fixed his gaze across the great room. Maiden placed her hands on his chest, and he readied himself for the journey.

"You do not command me, son." Light exploded from her palms, and Alek instantly tumbled backward.

His voice caught in his throat, and he remained on the floor in silent agony.

"As I said, you are not ready. If you cannot stop one of your mothers from knocking you to the ground, how are you to assist the Oracle?" she asked, staring down at him.

"Point taken," he squeaked.

"Now, on to more important matters." Maiden turned and took her place at the table. "The Oracle has a kind soul and is quite beautiful."

"These are matters you view to be more important than my returning to the Mortal Realm?" He got up slowly from the floor.

"You were almost defeated. Was that because of your desire to protect the humans? I do not seem to remember you being so fond of them."

"Yes, she *is* kind and beautiful," he groused, and flopped into the chair next to Maiden.

"As well as strong and brave. All impressive and important features for a young woman to possess," Maiden encouraged.

Alek averted his gaze from her probing stare.

"Do you not agree, my son?"

"All of my women have been great in some way."

"So Eva is no different than the mortal women who offered themselves to you so easily? I believe your comparison is grossly flawed. And you forget again that I am your mother. The one who carried and birthed you. Your true feelings have never been hidden from me."

Mother stopped rigidly at Alek's side. "I see you found her."

"Yes, although it wasn't a complicated task. Come, I did not properly greet you when I woke up." Relieved by the momentary break from Maiden's questioning, Alek enveloped Mother in an overenthusiastic hug.

Mother patted his back robotically. "I am glad you are doing so well."

"I'm much improved. Especially now that you are here."

"And you came at just the right time, sister. We were discussing Alek's adoration for the new Oracle." The apples of Maiden's cheeks turned pink.

"I wouldn't call it adoration, I only said—"

"It is that simple *feeling*," Mother interrupted, "that almost got you killed. I thought this had been handled. If it has not been, I suggest you exercise more control over your human-like emotions."

The rosy color drained from Maiden's face and she scowled at Mother before turning her attention back to Alek. "And to think I expected a more pleasant and compassionate response to our son's passions."

"Passions?" Alek's gaze darted between the two women. "Maiden, you're going too far. I never said—"

"Continue encouraging this nonsense, and next time you will not be able to rescue him from the doom he will inevitably face," Mother interjected.

"Quiet!" Alek slammed his fist on the stone table. "Do you not grow tired of this unending battle? Our home is dying, and the Mortal Realm suffers, yet you continue this incessant bickering."

"There is much about our past of which you are not aware," Maiden explained.

"None of that matters now. It's part of something that happened long ago, and there are greater threats to our present than your ghosts." Alek lurched over the table as nausea rolled through his stomach.

Immediately at his side, Maiden placed a warm hand on his back. "What is it, my son?" Her palm traced soothing circles between his shoulder blades.

"Sit, Alek. I will call Crone to rewrap your wound," Mother said.

"No." His hand shot out. "It's something else. There is something wrong."

Mother studied his face quizzically. "Crone found no other significant damage, internal or otherwise. Only scrapes and bruises, which have healed by now."

"You simply need rest. Come, I will take you back to your bedchamber," Maiden offered.

"No, something is wrong," he repeated. He rubbed at the dread resting beneath his sternum. "This feeling I carry is not for myself. It's unlike any other. I do not know how, but it's calling me to the Mortal Realm."

"Make haste to the Hall of Echoes. You must go now," Mother commanded.

Alek did as instructed, with the two Furies close behind. He rushed into the cavern and paused in the entryway as his eyes adjusted to the dark. "There's nothing here."

"Quickly, to the pool. Place your fingertips in its waters," Maiden urged.

"What is my intention? There is nothing I wish for it to show me."

"You are this realm's warrior. As your strength increases, so will your abilities and instincts," Mother said.

"Focus on the growing feeling within you. Your instincts will reveal to you what you need to know. That is one way we are able to call specific images to us. We have learned to trust ours, and you must do the same," Maiden coached.

"A warrior's instincts are his greatest tool," Mother added.

Alek knelt by the side of the lone puddle and dipped his fingers into the cool liquid. Waves rippled into a vivid and disturbing picture. Red streaks painted the snowy white walls of the image, and debris littered the blood-spattered floor.

"That looks like the hospital where Eva was taken after I defeated Alastor, but it was nothing like this before."

A scarlet cloud swirled through the hall, disappearing from sight but reemerging with every replay of the scene.

"The Nosoi!" Maiden gasped.

"You must not say such things, sister. You know as well as I that it has been locked away here with us for decades."

"Yes, but did you not see…."

"Hush, Maiden." Mother cleared the angst from her voice. "We will not give it power by uttering its name."

"Give what power?" The dread nestled within him increased as, for the first time, Alek saw fear in the stoic woman's eyes.

"Simply an evil that has long been vanquished. It is nothing with which you need be concerned. Now go. Your inner warrior has called you to this place for a purpose," Mother insisted.

"But remember, you are not fully healed or rested. You will require longer to recover if faced with battle," Maiden said.

"Understood." He nodded.

"Your time in the Mortal Realm will be short-lived. Do not force yourself to remain past your threshold, as you did before. Return home soon to regain your strength," Mother said.

As he stood, Alek instinctively felt for the crystal hanging around his neck. "My talisman," he whispered.

"It cracked upon your reentry," Maiden explained as she pulled the frayed leather cord from her pocket. "Half is with the Oracle, and half will remain with you."

Alek bent down so she could slip it over his head. "Will it still work with half of it missing?"

"Yes. When apart, each piece is strong, but together they are unstoppable." Maiden covered the fractured crystal with her palm. "The same could be said for you and the Oracle."

"Make contact with her. Together you will defeat

whatever is plaguing the Mortal Realm." Mother placed her hand over Maiden's.

"Goodbye, my son."

Alek wrestled his nerves while drifting weightlessly in the void between realms. He'd never felt such foreboding before a mission, or angst about the mortals he might run into. But Eva, she was something else. Realigning his focus with the task at hand, he envisioned the hospital. The ground firmed beneath his feet, and Alek readied himself for battle.

Thirteen

James allowed his mind to wander as his body twitched in deep relaxation.

"What are you thinking about?" Bridget yawned.

He could tell her the truth. Before opening his mouth, he imagined how the conversation would go down.

"Mel, my fiancée. But don't worry. She's dead."

Bridget would reply, "Oh, I'm sorry." People always said they were sorry.

"It's fine," he would lie. "I just realized you're the first person I've been with since her. Maybe it's a good thing it was with you and not some random girl."

He shrugged off the pretend exchange, and instead replied, "Nothing."

"Hey, do you hear buzzing?" Bridget lifted her head off his chest and sleepily looked around the room.

"Hear what?"

"Buzzing," she enunciated. "Do you hear it? It's been going on for awhile."

"Oh, shit. Yeah. What time is it?"

"No idea."

He rolled over and felt around for his vibrating phone. His head pulsed in the wake of Vodka James. He answered without looking at the screen. "Detective Graham."

"Hey Detective. You okay? I've been calling for the last five minutes straight."

"Yeah, Winslow, I'm fine. What's going on?"

"We're getting a bunch of strange calls from over at St. John's Hospital. There's a riot or something going on over there. They're in the process of dispatching a few cars, but as soon as the captain heard about it, he said he wanted you and Schilling to go check it out too." Phones trilled in the background as Winslow explained.

"A riot? How does that have anything to do with me?" James asked.

"It's not the riot as much as who may be behind it. The captain is thinking our two Mohawk Park suspects could be there, and he doesn't want them getting away again."

James sighed deeply. "I'm on my way. Have you already called Schilling?"

Winslow remained silent.

"Winslow, you called Schilling yet? Hello, Winslow? Hello?" James took the phone away from his ear. The red empty battery symbol flashed on the screen. "Shit," he cursed under his breath.

"Everything okay?" Bridget asked.

Goose bumps tickled his flesh as she marched her fingers up and down his naked back.

"Something's going on at the hospital. Captain's worried your friends are behind it."

"Eva? No way. What reason would she have to be at the hospital?"

He threw his legs over the side of the bed and pushed himself to standing. "No idea, but I have to do as I'm told." A smirk tipped the corner of his lip as he thought back to Bridget's sexy commands. His eyes traced her naked ivory body as she bent over and picked a shirt up off the floor.

"You sure you have to leave?" she asked.

"Yes, I'm sure. I'm definitely," he said, his gaze lingering on her, "definitely sure. I have to go."

Her hips swayed gently as she walked closer to him. "That's not what all of you is saying." She stood on her tiptoes and kissed him hungrily.

"You're making this hard for me."

"In more ways than one." Her grin stretched smoothly against his lips.

"Bridget, I have to go. If either Eva or Alek are there, it's best if I find them first."

"Ugh, you're right." She flopped onto the bed and teasingly stuck out her bottom lip. "Don't forget, you owe me dinner."

"Dinner?" His eyebrows lifted with the question.

"Yes, dinner. You know, sitting across from someone awkwardly while you both eat food and talk about stuff neither of you finds interesting. What, you thought we'd have sex and not go out on an official date?"

"Isn't that a little backwards?"

She picked up his briefs from where they'd landed catawampus on the bedside table and tossed them to him. "Well, you can't say I'm not interesting."

James slid on his pants and finished buttoning his

wrinkled shirt. "Uninteresting is definitely not a word I'd use to describe you."

"Then dinner it is. We need sustenance before round three anyway."

"Round three, huh?" Mel's face again swirled through his thoughts, uncorking a steady stream of guilt.

"Unless you're not interested."

"No, I am. I'm interested. I'll call you." He grabbed his keys off the dresser and darted out the front door.

· · ·

James parked his car outside the emergency room at St. John's and finished tucking in his shirt as he approached the sliding double doors. An ambulance sat a few feet from the entrance, its doors wide open and the engine humming steadily.

"Huh. That's strange," he mumbled, rounding the vehicle. Blood coated the ceiling and walls of the silver box, except for two streaks marking where the stretcher had been. He popped open the gun latch on his holster, and let his hand float above his Glock as he checked the front of the ambulance.

He remained tense as he cautiously walked through the sliding double doors and into the emergency room. The normally crowded waiting room was empty and silent. Droplets of blood speckled the floor, and upended chairs littered the room. Chills inched up James's spine as he thought back to all the apocalypse movies he'd seen with creepy scenes matching this one.

"Stop freaking out," he whispered, trying to calm himself. The phone rang from behind the abandoned check-in desk, and James's entire body flinched. "Shit!" he cursed.

He drew his gun and let it lead him through a set of swinging doors. Beeping machines and the low hum of equipment greeted him as he crept through the deserted treatment area. Beneath his feet, something crunched, and he attempted to maneuver around pages of medical charts and other hospital debris. He inched toward a blood-soaked curtain, moving it aside with his elbow before entering the makeshift room.

James's breath caught in his throat as he surveyed the scene. The ambulance stretcher sat in the middle of the room, and on it lay a body. A female, he assumed, given what she was wearing. Although without a face there was no way he could be sure. He holstered his weapon and forced himself to step closer, to look more intently at what he hadn't wanted to see at Tyson George's. The woman's facial features were gone. She no longer looked human; she was just an inside-out mess of muscle and bone. His stomach rolled, and he looked at the floor. Blood dripped from the stretcher, swirling together with another, larger pool coagulating on the tile. James's hand rested on his gun as he peered around the body. Slumped in the corner of the room was another corpse. An EMT, with strings of red muscle bursting from his face.

"Oh, fuck." James swallowed the bile building in his throat and hurried out of the room. He sucked in deep gulps of air and steadied himself against the countertop of the nurses' station.

A clatter erupted nearby, and James stiffened. He fought the urge to duck behind the counter, and instead removed his weapon from its holster. Every inch of his body vibrated with adrenaline. Silently, James rounded the nurses' station and inched closer to the noise. He reached a door marked "EMPLOYEES ONLY" and halted, listening carefully before barging in blind.

"Ouch! Shit!" a muffled voice shouted from behind the closed door.

The commotion continued, and James's hand lingered on the doorknob as he gathered his courage and assessed how many people were on the other side of the door.

"Must this happen every time?" the same deep voice seethed.

As sure as he could be that there was only one man in the room, James tore open the door and aimed his gun. "Police! Put your hands up!"

The man's muscles stretched the back of his shirt as he held his hands above his head and turned to face the detective.

"Alek?" James lowered his weapon, and stared blankly at the man he'd been hunting for days.

"Detective," Alek growled, and dropped his hands to his side. "I must warn you, you will not like what I will do if you try to apprehend me."

"I'll take my chances. Now raise your hands and come out slowly." He aligned the gun sight with Alek's chest, and stepped to the side to allow him room to exit the janitor's closet.

Alek set his jaw, but did as instructed. "You are lucky I must hold on to my strength for the real enemy."

James used his free hand to pat down Alek's pockets. "Oh yeah? And who's that?"

"This is a waste of time. I'm not here to be a part of one

of your petty human issues. I am only here to protect—" He stopped abruptly and furrowed his brow.

"To protect the Mortal Realm from evil? Yeah, Bridget told me all about you and your Underworld origins. That doesn't get you out of telling me what you're doing here. My petty human issue and your pretentious otherworldly bullshit have led us to the same place."

Alek eyeballed him skeptically. "Why do you not fear me?"

"I'm not scared of assholes. Never have been. Now tell me why you're here." He cocked his gun. "I won't ask again."

Alek took a deep breath. "The floating red mist. I believe it's responsible for this destruction. That's why I have come. To find the cause."

"Floating mist." James recalled the video of Tyson. "Okay, but you stick with me. Try anything, and I'll shoot you. I know you won't die, but it'll fucking hurt." He holstered his gun. "You need to see this." He led Alek to the bodies, but paused outside the red curtain. "I'll wait here. Don't touch anything." He pulled open the fabric and let it shield his face from what he'd already seen.

Alek's shoes squeaked on the floor as he walked through ruby puddles. "How did this happen?"

"I was hoping you could tell me. Until today, I'd never seen anything like it before."

Alek appeared from the room, his expression unchanged. "We must locate the source before it's able to do this to another mortal."

"Then let's get after it. Follow me."

Veins bulged from Alek's meaty arm as he slammed it against James's chest, holding him back. "I am an immortal.

It's best you stay behind me."

"If you want to serve as my semi-human shield, be my guest, but we need to take the stairs. We don't know what's happening on the rest of the floors, and I'd rather not get stuck in an elevator while weird and dangerous shit is happening."

"Agreed. I don't trust those floating boxes."

James followed Alek into the stairwell and matched his brisk pace up the steps. "He'd be bitching all the way, but now would be a good time to have my partner. I can trust him."

"You and I are not partners." Alek paused outside the door leading to the second floor and peered through its narrow window.

"And every comment isn't about you," James quipped. "There might be officers in the building. You see any uniforms?"

"I see nothing. Only a corridor."

"Okay, here's what we're going to do." He gripped his gun, and double-checked there was a round in the chamber before continuing. "Open the door slowly. I'll go in and clear the hall. I'll call to you once I do, and we'll proceed to sweep the rest of the floor. Got it?"

"Or," Alek said, throwing open the door, "we can advance as I would."

A guttural howl emanated from the end of the hall. Alek turned toward the noise, his eyes wide. James raised his gun and braced himself for whatever was coming.

"Dammit, Alek," James hissed.

Alek tumbled back and spilled into the stairwell. Howls turned to shrieks as the man who tackled him snarled and clawed at the immortal. The attacker's hospital gown hung from his neck, and vanilla boils bubbled up from his exposed back.

James gathered his wits and aimed his gun at the man.

"I do not require your assistance," Alek grunted as he wrapped his hands around the man's head and yanked. The body immediately went limp, and the shrieks turned to wet burbles. Alek rolled the corpse off of him. "It is taken care of." He wiped his hands on his jeans and got to his feet.

James's stomach sank. "You fucking killed him. You broke his neck and killed him."

"And what would you have done with that?" Alek nodded toward James's firearm.

"Not killed him, that's for sure. At least not without trying to subdue him first. We're not doing this your way anymore."

"I achieved the goal. He no longer poses a threat," Alek said matter-of-factly.

"Alek…." James's voice faded into a whisper as he watched the bruised and bloody body shake violently against the stairs.

"What? Do you fear me now, mortal?"

The video of Tyson flashed through James's thoughts as he struggled to take his eyes off the contorting figure. *The cloud. It comes next.*

"Alek, move!" James pulled the immortal through the open door and kicked it shut behind them. Scarlet flecks beat against the window and disappeared as rapidly as they came. "That shit is alive!" James scrambled backward until he hit the wall. "It just tried to fucking attack us! What the fuck does it want?"

"I don't know," Alek said. "But it is a creature that does not belong here."

"Well, no shit." James collected his gun from the floor and ran a shaking hand through his hair. "But I've seen it before. That same flying cloud, or floating mist, or whatever the fuck it is. There are two bodies down at the morgue. One with a blown-out face because of that same red shit, and the other, his wife. They said they're not sure who killed her, but judging by that freak in the hospital gown, my bet is on the husband."

Alek stretched his neck and peered down the hall. "Quiet!" he commanded. "I hear footsteps."

"Good. Maybe it's someone who can tell us what the fuck is going on," James murmured.

"Help! Oh, God, somebody help me!" Frantic pleas and thundering footsteps hit James before he saw anyone. He raised his pistol and readied himself for whoever, whatever, was barreling around the corner.

"Shoot them! Shoot them!" a young man dressed in blue nurse's scrubs wailed as he sprinted toward Alek and James.

Four wild-eyed, snarling doctors were hard on his heels. Pinkish foam sprayed from their mouths as they snapped and clawed at the empty space between them and their target's pale flesh. James's heart thundered ferociously as the twisted scene registered as reality.

"Do it now!" the man squealed as he approached.

James took aim at the leader of the pack, a slender woman. With the barrel of his gun focused on her right shoulder, he pulled the trigger. The bullet tore through the meat of her arm, twisting her torso and slowing her down, but only momentarily.

James fired again, this time striking her knee. Her leg buckled, and she fell into a forward roll, then sprang to her feet again.

The man glanced behind him before shouting, "Shoot her in the head!"

James pointed the gun at the face of his moving target, but couldn't make himself pull the trigger. "A little help here, immortal," he said, holding on to the remaining fibers of his composure.

With the speed and ferocity of a lion, Alek charged the herd, knocking three of them over like bowling pins.

"Find Eva!" Alek grunted as he pushed his shoulder into the three rabid doctors, forcing them down the hall and away from James and the nurse.

James took off, matching the rapid pace of the man being chased. He pushed open the first windowless door he saw and yanked the nurse in after him. "Don't let them open this," he commanded, pinning the man's narrow shoulders against the wood.

"Okay," the man squeaked as the fourth crazed doctor began to pelt the door with her fists.

James rushed to the corner of the room, picked up a plastic chair, and darted back to the door. "When I say go, you move. Got it?"

The young man nodded frantically.

"Okay. Ready, go!"

He stepped out of the way, and James jammed the back of the chair under the door handle. Apprehensively, he let go of the arms. The chair shook against the hollow thuds emanating from the other side of the door.

James felt around for the empty bed behind him and

sat back onto the spongy mattress. Panic ignited every muscle in his body, and he let its power rush through his trembling extremities.

"What's happening to them?" the nurse asked through his tears.

James kept his gaze glued to the door. "I don't know."

"Do—do you have backup coming?"

"I don't know," James said flatly.

"Well, do you know how to stop them?"

"I know as much as you do about this whole fucking thing!" James barked.

The nurse inhaled sharply, and James really looked at him for the first time since he'd come barreling down the hall. The nurse had tucked his short legs under his chin and sat in a tight ball by the head of the bed. The left half of his head was shaved, revealing small silver studs that climbed up his ear lobe. His cheeks glistened with fresh tears, and fear nestled in his dark eyes.

They sat in silence for a moment, listening to the guttural bellows and repeated sharp thuds on the other side of door.

"I'm glad I ran into you. Thank you for helping me." The nurse's voice came out as a whisper, and he cleared his throat before continuing. "They would've killed me. I already saw them do it once." He adjusted his bedazzled lanyard and tucked the shaggy side of his charcoal hair behind his ear. "Do you think your friend is going to be okay?"

"Friend?" James scoffed. "I wouldn't call him that, but yeah. He'll be fine. He has a bit of an unfair advantage."

"I think we could use that right now. What is it?"

"Wait." James held his hand up and listened. "Do you hear that?"

"Hear what?"

"Exactly." He noiselessly slid off the bed and pressed his ear against the door. "I think she's gone. Come on. Let's get out of here before any of them have a chance to come back."

"We can't go out there." He grabbed James's sleeve. "What if one of them is on the other side of the door waiting for us?"

"We can't stay in here. It's only a matter of time before they're able to break through this door. Unless you want to try jumping out that window, I suggest we make a run for it while we have the opportunity."

He looked at the window, cringed, and looked back at James. "Okay. When we get out of here, take a right. There's another stairwell at the end of the hall that has street access. Plus, there are no patient rooms down that way, so there shouldn't be any more of those *people*," he said with a shudder.

"Got it. You ready to make a run for it?"

His eyes widened and he nodded slowly. "No."

"Good. On the count of three. I'll lead." James exhaled sharply. "One, two, three."

Fourteen

Electricity seared Eva's arms as the ground hardened under her feet. The sulfurous odor of burning hair filled her nostrils, and she held out her arms to steady herself against the fumes wafting up from her own body.

A shrill squeal pierced her ears. Then came the shouting. "Get the fuck out of my room!"

"Bridge, it's me." Eva slowly and painfully dodged a barrage of red-bottomed shoes. "Ouch. Dammit. Bridget, stop! It's just me."

"Get out! Get out! Get out!" Bridget shrieked.

"You're going to mess up your shoes!" Eva shouted over her best friend's squeaky yips.

The onslaught of soaring high heels ended, and Bridget's blonde head poked out of the closet. "Eva? Jesus fucking Christ! You scared the shit out of me!" She raised a black pump above her head, and Eva recoiled. "Oh no!" Bridget sucked in air and hurried over to her friend. "I hope I didn't hurt any of them."

Bridget scooped up the shoes and gently lowered them onto the bed. "Oh my God. Are you okay? Here," she said, pushing over a bit of the pile, "lay down. What happened? Your outfit is destroyed, and you're all blistery. Well, kind of. I mean, you seem to be healing super fast, so that's a good thing, but you're still all splotchy and burned." The last word came out in a whisper.

"I'll be fine in a little bit. As soon as I heal completely. But it definitely hurts right now, and bad." She stared down at her tattoo. A large blister covered where the branches once were, but the broad, black trunk of the family tree Alastor had marked her with remained unharmed. She rubbed at the base of the tree sprouting up from her wrist, and watched as the injured skin replaced itself with new skin, the thick, onyx ink resurfacing. She quelled the visions of Alastor, the basement, Alek, and asked, "Why are you whispering?"

"I don't know. I'm trying to be sensitive. Okay, let's think. What helps heal stuff? Oh, I know! Neosporin. You need the first aid kit! Be right back," Bridget said, cheerily bounding out of the room.

Eva closed her eyes and leaned back against the mound of unorganized pillows. "Just relax. Everything's going to be fine. You're back in the real world now. Alek's alive. You're a powerful Oracle. Everything's fine. Just be positive and kind to yourself, like Maiden said."

"Okay, I'm back, and I have just the thing to get you all normal again." The bed slouched as Bridget took a seat next to her. "Oh, well shit. I'm too late. You seem to be getting better at that."

Eva opened her eyes and examined her exposed skin. The wounds had closed, leaving behind pale pink patches of fresh and tender epidermis.

"At least I can do this now." Bridget opened her arms and wrapped them around Eva, squeezing her gently. "I've missed you!" she squealed. "Everyone's been so worried. Me, your mom, James…." She released Eva and tilted her head to the side. Her chest-length curls slid off her back and bounced loosely at her shoulders. "Gah, when did 'everyone' become me, your mother, and a detective? You really need to get out more. Wait, how did you even get in here?" Her eyes widened, and a smile curled her sparkly coral lips. "You discovered another one of your crazy super powers, didn't you? Oh my god, you did! You know, you should really write all this stuff down and turn it into, like, your memoirs or something someday. Then, some big-shot producer will make it into a movie. I wonder who they'll get to play me? I'm thinking Gigi Hadid. Do you think she knows how to act?"

Eva grabbed her babbling friend by the shoulders and steadied her. "Bridget, slow down. Alek's mothers sent me back after I started sparking all over the place like some kind of defective firework. Apparently human bodies aren't made to go to Tartarus. Not living ones, anyway. Who knew?" She shrugged.

"That's a relief. Not the thing about you being sparky, just the part where you were magically transported here. I'm already packing to go to a hotel. That's why my shoes were so available. They were going in my suitcase next." She motioned to the heels piled on the corner of the bed. "Ever since James stopped by earlier today totally unannounced, I didn't want to take the chance of him or anyone else just thinking they could pop over. But not you, of course. You're invited anytime. And, now that I think about it, James can come back too. Yeah, I'd really like it if he'd *come* again, if you get my meaning. And he's not too old, if that's what you were thinking. So, I've changed my mind. I'm going to stay here."

"Wait, you had sex with Detective Graham? Seriously, Bridget. You've got to be kidding me. How long was I gone?"

"Not long. Like, a day or something. And James is one of the good guys now. *Really* good." She grinned.

"Bridget, he pointed a gun at me and was 100 percent going to shoot. There's no way he's on our team, and you can't turn someone away from the dark side with your vagina. That's not how it works."

Bridget rolled her eyes and exhaled sharply. "I don't think he actually would have shot you. But none of that matters now, because I told him everything that's going on, and he *is* on our side. Promise. Plus, you can fix a lot of problems by using your lady bits. You'd know that if you ever freed yours from your clothes."

Eva shook her head, ignoring her friend's last comment. "What do you mean you told him everything?"

"I mean, all the stuff about Tartarus. Well, all the stuff I could remember anyway. And about how you're the Oracle and you're working for the forces of good with Alek, who's some Thor-like immortal warrior guy sent from the Underworld to fight monsters and banish them back to Hell jail."

"And he actually believed you? Did you have your clothes on or off when you said all this?"

"On!" she said, playfully hitting Eva's arm. "But now that I think about it, it probably would've gone over better

if I'd done it the other way. God, James is all sorts of sexy."
She fanned herself and batted her impossibly long eyelashes.
"The man knows how to use his tongue. And that body.
Every inch of it was rock hard. The farthest thing you can
get from a flabby Dad bod."

Laughter shook Eva's core for the first time in days.
"Well, I guess I should congratulate you on adding another
handsome victim to your list."

Bridget beamed. "Thank you."

"But just because you ended up in bed with him doesn't
mean he believed you."

"Yeah, but do you not remember vanishing from the
middle of Mohawk Park? James was there, and that's not
something he could have missed. It would make anyone start
asking questions. Oh, and then there's this." She grabbed her
laptop from the bedside table, and moved her finger across
the track pad until the screen illuminated. She clicked on
the e-mail icon and scrolled through her unopened mail.
"Sorry to get straight down to weird Oracle business, but
after some seriously amazing convincing on my part, James
forwarded this video to me, and I told him I'd show it to you
the second I saw you again." She found the e-mail, opened
the attachment, and paused before moving the arrow to the
play button. "Just a quick disclaimer, it's from a crime scene,
so you're going to see someone die. I guess that was also sort
of a spoiler. Oh well. Ready?" She pressed play before Eva
had a chance to process the information and answer.

Eva cringed as she watched the graphic footage. "Wait,
can you play it again? But just the very last part, right after
he jumps."

Bridget skipped backward and again pressed play.

"Okay, pause it." The image froze on the scarlet swarm hovering over the mutilated body. "I feel like I've seen this before."

"How? James only got a copy of it today, and I'm pretty sure this guy died less than forty-eight hours ago."

"No, not this exact video, but a picture of something really similar." Eva scooted off the end of the bed and paced in front of Bridget's dresser. "Where the hell did I see it?"

"The Internet?" Bridget offered.

"No, it was in a book, but I can't remember which one." Eva dug her toes into the carpet and stared down at the fluffy fibers surrounding her feet.

"Some book that must've been. With pictures like that, I would have had nightmares for weeks," Bridget mumbled.

"That's it!" Eva said with a clap. "Books that gave me nightmares. Come on, Bridge. We need that book, which means we need to break into my house." Flooded with enthusiasm, Eva rushed to Bridget's closet in search of appropriate burglar attire.

FIFTEEN

"Wait, wait, wait, wait, wait," Bridget said, waving her hands in front of her face. "Did your trip to the Underworld scramble your brain? Because there's absolutely no way you can break into your house."

"Of course there is. It is *my* house, after all." Eva disappeared into the vast walk-in closet.

"Yeah, but you're a wanted fugitive. Remember what happened last time we tried to ignore what was going on in the world and go out?" Bridget leaned against the doorframe and crossed her arms over her chest. "I got arrested. Arrested, Eva. There were bruises around my wrists, the building smelled like depression and Kraft singles, and, worst of all, *I* had to pay for all of the damage to that rental car I smashed into the police cruiser. Me! Can you even believe it? That crappy SUV sucked up my fun-things-Bridget-likes-to-go-do money for the next month."

Eva pulled a black T-shirt over her head before answering. "You should have gotten the extra rental insurance."

"Jesus Christ. Now you sound like my mother," Bridget mumbled. "Why are you changing into that boring black top? My closet has so much more to offer."

"Yeah, but nothing particularly practical." She grabbed an electric blue, fringed skirt from its hanger and offered it as evidence. "I'd be spotted immediately wearing anything else, and what if I have to make another run for it?" Eva dug through one of the cedar-lined drawers and pulled out a pair of black yoga pants.

"You'd think with how much they charged me for this condo, they'd have figured out how to infuse the drawers with vanilla or something. I don't know how stealthy you're going to be when you smell like a hamster cage," Bridget commented.

"You mean, how stealthy *we're* going to be." Eva threw a pair of black pants and matching black top at Bridget and followed her back into the bedroom. "Put those on. It's almost dark, so we need to get going."

"Fine," Bridget moaned, and slid her pastel pink shorts halfway off before flopping onto the bed. The TV clicked on and the screen flared to life. "Oh, *there's* the remote," she said, fishing it out from between the tangled bed sheets.

"As you can see, we're a few blocks away from St. John's Hospital." The newscaster pointed behind her as she began her live coverage.

"The news again," Bridget whined. "This shit is always on."

Eva slowly stepped into a pair of black sweats as she listened to the unfolding news story.

"Police barricades have been set out in a mile radius around the location. It still remains unclear what exactly is happening tonight at one of Tulsa's busiest midtown hospitals, but I have been informed that lives have been lost in the events transpiring in the building behind me. I'll keep you up-to-date with more information as soon as it is available."

"Are you finished watching this, or do you want me to leave it on in the hope they'll flash a picture of you on-screen along with the Tulsa's Most Wanted headline?" Bridget quipped.

"Yeah, turn it off. We need to leave anyway."

"But it is nice to see there's something else going on in this town that doesn't involve you."

"It is refreshing, isn't it?" Eva smiled and stuffed her feet into a pair of Bridget's tennis shoes.

"Actually, James is at that hospital right now, making sure you're not at the scene."

"That's funny and kind of nerve-racking at the same time."

"So, you know I love these little adventures we go on, but how do you think we're going to get into your house unnoticed? I doubt your mom will be enjoying a night out on the town while her daughter is missing and being hunted by the law."

"We both know that house inside and out. We'll develop a solid plan as soon as we assess the situation."

"Your college sentences may make you sound smart, but I know that's just another way of saying that you have zero fucking idea." Bridget held up her hand. "Look, whatever. We'll assess and figure out something brilliant, I'm sure." She grabbed a pair of black flats and slipped them on her pristinely manicured feet. "Wouldn't this be easier if we stopped by B&N or the library, and picked up the book there instead of ninjaing our way into your house?"

"I doubt any store or library is going to have the book I'm looking for. It was my grandmother's. There's not one like it anywhere," Eva explained.

"Then we should get in touch with Alek and have him poof himself into your house, grab the book, then poof himself back here. That'd save everyone some time, and you wouldn't be risking anything. Where is he anyway?"

"He's still in Tartarus," Eva said quietly. "He got hurt, really hurt, trying to find me after I ran. He would have died if his mother hadn't pulled him back home."

"He'll be okay though, right?"

"Yeah, yeah he'll be fine. Full recovery expected. And something good did come out of my trip. I now have these." She masked the overwhelming guilt fluttering within her with a fake grin as she pulled the thin vial and the crystal from her bra. "Tada!" she exclaimed, holding them up for Bridget to inspect.

"Oh, hmm." Bridget wrinkled her nose. "The crystal's cute, but the one with the water in it looks like something you'd get from the gift shop at the aquarium."

"The crystal is part of Alek's talisman, which gives him the ability to travel between realms. Apparently, I need to have a piece of him close to me or bad stuff will happen. I don't really understand. And this is water from the Galazoneri." She stretched out the word, trying to enunciate it correctly. "It's how the Furies communicate between the levels of the Underworld. Like a realm chat, I guess. It's supposed to give me the ability to call Tartarus. Or at least that's how Maiden explained it." She tucked the items back under her shirt.

"If they're both important, and they sound like they are, you shouldn't trust them to the abyss of your bra. That's only for your gloss, cards, and ID when we're out dancing or drinking." Bridget pulled open the top drawer of her dresser and fished through its contents. "Here." She held up a delicate gold chain. "Put them on this so they don't accidentally bounce free of your jumbo tatas if you have to make a quick getaway."

Eva strung the items on the chain and slipped it over her head. "Thanks, Bridge."

"Always here to help. Although, you're definitely going to have to explain who this Maiden person is and what exactly happened in Tartarus. I'm dying to know what kind of fashion is going on down there. And if it was all on fire with people moaning and begging for mercy." Bridget smiled and clapped her hands.

"The strangest things make you happy."

Bridget cocked her head to the side. "Well, if you went to Spain I'd be excited to hear about the Spanish. It's sort of the same thing."

Eva shook her head. "No, no it's not. But I'll tell you everything on our way to my house." She pointed to the lavishly draped window. "The sun is down. Let's get this show on the road."

"Thelma and Louise ride again!" Bridget hollered, punching her fist in the air.

• • •

"Get down! Get down!" Bridget hissed as she turned off of Fifteenth Street and into Eva's neighborhood.

Eva immediately bent over and rested her head on her knees. "What is it? Did you see my mom?"

"No, there were just a lot of cops guarding a barricade on that street, and I got really nervous all of a sudden." Bridget wrung her hands, then placed them back on the steering wheel. "The anxiety is killing me. I need a Xanax with a champagne chaser."

Eva sat up in her seat and huffed. "You have to relax. You can't be more on edge than I am. You're supposed to be the calm one in this situation."

"I'm trying, but you could go to jail, and I—"

"Hush! You're going to jinx us." She scanned the line of parked cars and pointed to an empty spot. "Park over there. We'll walk the rest of the way."

"So," Bridget whispered, as she piled her wavy hair on top of her head and fastened it in a messy bun. "How are we going to do this?"

Eva slid out of the passenger seat and met her friend on the sidewalk. "You don't have to whisper yet, Bridge. We're like, four blocks away." Nervously, she tugged down the bill of her hat to shield her face from the flickering light of the streetlamp.

"I'm trying to prep myself for stealth mode." Bridget increased the volume of her whisper. "What's the plan?"

"Uh, I don't really have one yet. I figured we'd get closer and see if my mom's home. Then," Eva said, shrugging, "I don't know. Go from there?"

Bridget shook her head back and forth. Wisps of hair floated down into her face. "Shitty, shitty, shitty, shitty plan. Come on. Follow me."

Eva kept to the shadows and let Bridget forge a path.

Unfamiliar houses surrounded her, and Eva realized she was lost in her own neighborhood.

"I must drive on autopilot," she murmured, really looking at the houses for the first time.

"Almost there," Bridget muttered.

"Finally. I feel like we've been walking for at least half an hour, and we didn't park that far away."

"We've been taking the long way around to get to your house. You've never gone this way? I've done it at least a thousand times."

They turned down Columbia Avenue and Eva relaxed at the familiarity of her surroundings. "Shouldn't we be one street over? We're going to end up behind my house."

"Oh my God." Bridget let out an exasperated sigh. "Would you just trust me and stop asking so many questions? I've totally got this." She stopped in front of a quaint, Craftsman-style home and inspected the outside. The white siding glowed pale blue in the moonlight. "Looks good," she chirped, before traipsing through the grass and into the backyard.

Eva cemented her feet to the ground. "Bridget! We can't be back there. That is someone's backyard."

"What did I say about trusting me? Plus, they don't have a fence," she said matter-of-factly. "And all the lights in the house are off. It's not that late, so they're probably not even home."

"But that doesn't mean we can go back there whenever we want. It's not our house."

"I love you, but sometimes you're like an annoying little sister." Bridget marched over to Eva, grabbed her arm, and pulled her through the yard. "Would it make you feel better if I told you I'd asked the people who live here if I could climb their fence whenever I needed to?" Bridget put a foot on the wood and hefted herself up on the first rung.

Eva followed her lead and did the same. "You really asked them?"

"Well, no. But how else do you think I got into your house all those times when I was drunk in high school and couldn't go home?"

"I guess I was under the absurd assumption that you used the front door." Eva peered over the fence and studied the backyard. Circles of colorful light glowed from the solar-powered glass balls Lori was so fond of. Together, they'd chosen the perfect location for each orb and giddily awaited nightfall, when the backyard would be transformed into a disco-like oasis. There was a world full of memories trapped within the confines of the fence. A world in which Eva felt like she no longer belonged.

"It doesn't look like your mom's here," Bridget said, interrupting Eva's thoughts.

Eva blinked back tears and swallowed through the tightness building in her throat. "You're right. I don't see any of the usual lights on."

"Well, let's get this done before she comes back." Bridget hoisted her slender frame over the fence and stuck the landing on the other side. "What are you waiting for?" she asked, tucking a few free strands of hair behind her ears. "Just climb the last two step things and jump. It's only cushy grass down here." She bounced up and down a few times to demonstrate its cushiness.

Eva did as Bridget instructed, and climbed the two wooden planks before hopping over the top of the fence.

"Oof!" Air rushed out of her lungs as she smacked down onto the grass. "Not so cushy," she croaked.

"Good thing you heal quickly." Bridget offered Eva her hand and pulled her to her feet.

"Doesn't make it hurt any less," she groaned, wiping dirt and grass from her pants.

"Is it weird being back? I mean, you haven't been gone for very long, but so much has changed."

Sadness rippled beneath her chest as Eva studied the back of her house. "I feel like the girl who lived here doesn't even exist anymore."

Bridget interlaced her fingers with Eva's and gently squeezed her hand. "When the Lord closes a door, somewhere He opens a window."

"Are you quoting *The Sound of Music?*"

"It's the most positive thing I could think of. You know I'm not good with emotions. It would've been better if I'd burst into song with 'My Favorite Things,' but I figured someone would call animal control, thinking cats were being slaughtered."

Eva controlled her giggles and hopped up the steps behind her. "Dammit. I don't have my key."

"No problem. Mine's around here somewhere." Bridget stood on her tippy toes and felt around the top of the doorframe.

"Bridge, you don't have a key."

"Voila!" she cheered, and slipped it into the lock.

"Since when has that been there?"

Bridget shrugged. "Since your mom asked me to house-sit back when we were, like, twelve or something." She put the key back in its spot and slowly pushed the door open.

The distinctive *ding* of the alarm sounded, and Bridget let the door swing open the rest of the way. "Alarm's on. That means no one's home."

Eva jogged to the keypad and entered her code. "Okay. Mom packed up all of Grandma's books and put them in the closet in the spare room upstairs. All we have to do is find the box, then leave the way we came in."

"Easy peasy," Bridget chimed.

"Yeah, except that it's dark, and we can't see anything since we can't turn on any of the lights."

Bridget made a few clicks on her phone and a blinding fluorescent light shot Eva in the face. "We have light now."

Eva held onto the railing as she walked upstairs, blinking the white bursts from her vision.

"I'm so glad Lululemon finally opened a store here. Your butt looks amazing in those pants, by the way. It's probably all the running you've been doing lately. You should really keep it up." Bridget poked Eva's cheeks.

"A firm ass. At least there's one pro to being wanted by the police." They reached the second floor, and Eva paused before continuing down the dark hallway. "Bridge, hand me the light." Eva took control of Bridget's phone and headed toward the guest bedroom's closed door.

Bridget's words tickled the back of Eva's neck. "I'm so nervous. Aren't you nervous?"

"Yeah, but only because you're making me nervous by spider monkeying me." A chill sprouted in her spine, and she shook her shoulders. "There's nothing to be nervous about, Bridge. It's just my house. It's not like there's going to be some crazy axe murderer hiding under the bed."

"Well there probably will be now that you said

that," Bridget hissed.

Eva rolled her eyes and threw open the door. The narrow beam of light barely reached the opposite wall as she shone it around the room. A quilt-covered bed and two end tables were packed tightly against the wall across from the closet and a towering armoire. "See? Nothing bad." Eva walked through the cramped space and opened the closet door.

"Not nothing." Bridget fanned the air in front of her face. "It smells like old people in here."

"This was my yiayiá's room. All of her stuff is packed up in this closet. No one comes in here, and it hasn't changed much since she passed. And, luckily for us, my mom has some kind of OCD when it comes to labeling things."

The white light illuminated Lori's neat handwriting on the side of each box. "Books" was written in bold, black sharpie on two of them. "Of course they have to be on the bottom," Eva sighed. "Come help me with these. You're being a horrible sidekick."

Bridget moaned and dragged herself over to the open closet. "You know I'm not good at manual labor."

"Put all those hours you spend working out with your hot trainer to good use and lift up these boxes for me. They're just full of clothes, and Yiayiá wasn't big, so they shouldn't be too heavy."

"You really think my trainer's hot?" She squatted down and dug her fingers in between the two boxes. "I didn't even give him that much time. I was like, meh, beige paint."

"Just lift when I tell you." Eva positioned herself next to Bridget and gripped the sides of the second cardboard box. "Okay, go." The weight lifted from the top of the box, and Eva slid it free from the stack. "Perfect. Only one more."

Bridget released the boxes, and they collided with the floor with a soft thud. She shuffled over and readied herself for another round. "If I break a nail because of this, I'm seriously going to be pissed."

"Lift," Eva instructed, ignoring Bridget's whines. She yanked the second box free and slid it next to the first. "You open that one, I'll open this one," she said, grabbing the phone and shining the light over the two boxes.

"Why don't we just take both of them with us and sort it out once we get back to my place?" Bridget asked.

"Do you want to have to carry an extra twenty pounds for no reason?"

"Right." Bridget tore through the cracked packing tape and opened the cardboard flaps. "Any of these the book you're looking for?"

Eva peered into the box and dug through the unorganized piles of paperbacks. "Nope. All of them are just regular, everyday books." She scooted over to the second box and used her free hand to peel off the tape.

"Well what's the difference between your book and a regular book?"

"This," Eva whispered as she uncovered the pile. Cracked leather bound the oversized pages of each of the four books nestled in the box.

"Whoa. That looks like some serious reading."

"Yeah, and I didn't realize there was more than one. Let's put that box back in the closet, and get this one to your car before my mom comes home."

"I can't believe this actually worked out," Bridget grunted as she hefted the box on top of the others. "This whole thing has been way more intense and exciting than when I used to hide bottles of vodka in your room."

"We're not in the clear yet." Eva handed Bridget her phone, and lifted the bulky box. "Wait, you used to hide liquor in my room? What if my mom had found it and I got in trouble?"

Bridget closed the door behind them and led the way down the hall. "She'd never have believed they were yours anyway. You barely drink even now."

Safely at the bottom of the stairs, Bridget switched off the flashlight and tucked her phone into her pocket. "You want to take that out back while I set the alarm and lock up, or—"

"Shh!" Eva interrupted. "Do you hear that?"

Murmurs wafted in from the front of the house as Lori's silhouette closed in on the front door.

"Shit!" Bridget squeaked and ducked behind the banister. "What do we do?"

"Crap!" Eva gasped. "You can see straight through to the backyard from the front door. There's no way I can make it over the fence before she gets inside. I have to hide."

Bridget poked her head out from behind the swirly wooden railing. "You have to hide? What about me?"

"You need to do what you do best and create a distraction. Think of it as a lesson in acting. Get enough practice in, and maybe you'll be playing yourself in my memoir's movie adaptation."

Bridget stood, her eyes widening. "Oh my god. What a great point!" She dug in her pocket, pulled out a jangly clump of keys, and dropped them on top of the box. "I'll meet you at the car as soon as I'm finished winning this Oscar."

The deadbolt clicked, and Eva hurried into the kitchen.

The pantry door hung open, and she pushed the box into the small space before squeezing in behind it. She tried closing the door, but the toes of her tennis shoes stuck out about an inch too far. She shuffled as far away from the sliver of moonlight spilling in from the open door as possible and prayed Bridget's acting skills were up to par. The front door creaked open, and Eva held her breath and waited.

"Bridget, what are you doing here?" Lori's voice filled Eva with longing and regret.

"I am so sorry that I broke in, Ms. K. I hope you can forgive me. I just—I wanted to be closer to my best friend, since she's not here. I—I'm worried about her." Bridget's voice cracked, and she let out a haggard sigh. "And I want her to come home. I thought if I came here, it would make me feel better. But I also didn't want to bother you. I know you're going through so much right now."

"Oh, Bridget. You're no bother at all. And I understand how you feel. Sometimes I sit up in her room. I picture her coming home, sitting next to me, telling me about her day, the boring classes she's in, and all of this fades away like some kind of horrible nightmare." Lori's voice drifted away into a long pause. "But there's no reason for you to be sorry. You're welcome here anytime. Like you always have been."

Eva wept silently in the closet.

"Thanks, Ms. K. That means a lot."

"Now, why don't we go into the kitchen? I'll make us some nice chamomile tea, and we can talk about what else has been going on in your world. It will be good for both of us," Lori said.

Eva went rigid, and half-conceived excuses tumbled through her head as she raced to choose one before Lori found her hiding place.

"Actually, I'd like it a lot better if we just stayed in the living room." Panic momentarily increased Bridget's volume, and she chuckled nervously. "I mean, the kitchen is great and all, but it doesn't have a couch, and couches are comfortable. Don't you think?"

"Then I'll just get the water going and come back in here. You don't take honey in your tea, do you?"

"Oh no, oh no, oh no." Eva squeezed her eyes shut and tried to tuck herself deeper into the pantry. "Come on, Bridget. Hurry up and stop her."

"I uh—I uh—I—" A loud thud rattled through the house's first floor.

"Oh God! Bridget!"

Eva opened her eyes, and waited a few moments before slipping out of the pantry. Quietly, she tiptoed passed the refrigerator and leaned into the opening to the living room. Bridget lay sprawled out on the wood floor, Lori gently caressing her blonde curls. "I owe you, Bridge," Eva breathed before pulling herself away from the doorway. She darted back to the pantry and lifted the box and maneuvered to the backdoor. She wanted desperately to run to her mother, bury her head in her shoulder, and tell her everything that had happened. Instead, she silently opened the door and left only a whisper. "Bye Mom. I'll be back soon. I love you."

SIXTEEN

James was ready to outrun whatever creature they might encounter beyond the safety of the exam room. He took a deep breath and prepared his legs to quickly carry him to the exit.

"Wait!"

James stopped centimeters short of pulling the chair away from the door.

"I said to turn right, but I meant left. Turn left."

"To the left at the end of the hall."

The nurse nodded confidently.

"To the left at the end of the hall," James repeated, so his body would move on autopilot. "Easy enough." He gripped the chair and readied himself for the mad dash to freedom.

"Before we go out there, I should tell you that I'm not a fighter. No, that's a lie. I've been in a few fights, but I've never actually won, or fought back, really."

"Look," James said, glancing down at the nurse's nametag. "Patrick."

"It's PJ, actually."

"Okay, PJ. Don't worry. There's not going to be any fighting. We're going to go down the hall and exit the building like you said. We are going to run, though. You think you can handle that?"

"Yes. I have short legs, but I'm very fast."

James didn't give PJ another chance to stall him. Instead, he jerked the chair away from the door and grabbed the handle. He cracked open the door and surveyed the immediate vicinity. "All clear." He shuffled into the corridor and motioned for PJ to follow.

Together, they turned left and bolted to the end of the hall.

"Now where?" James flattened his back against the wall and waited for PJ to further direct him.

"Now we go right." PJ peered around the corner and froze. "Holy cow. You really killed her," he whispered.

James stepped around PJ and looked down the hall. The slender doctor sat slumped against the exit door like a forgotten doll.

"Yeah, I guess I really did," James muttered somberly.

"I don't see anyone else. Can we make a run for it?" PJ asked.

James readied himself and his weapon for action. "Let's go. I got your back."

PJ took off around the corner, but came to an abrupt stop a few feet in front of the doctor.

"What are you doing?" James pressed his back against PJ's, and maintained a sweeping visual survey of the hallway.

The muscles in PJ's back tightened. "I—I don't think your gun is what killed her."

James glanced at the body, and immediately understood PJ's trepidation. "It's fine. Go around her. Everything's fine."

"But it's not. Her—her face. It's gone."

James shoved his gun in its holster and turned PJ around to face him. "Keep an eye on the hall. If you see anything, let me know immediately."

PJ swallowed hard and nodded stiffly. "Okay."

James hurried to the doctor and forced his hands to grip her ankles. A slick red streak followed her head as it slid down the door and onto the floor. He couldn't take his eyes off her face as he shuffled hesitantly backward. It was the same as Tyson's. The same as the girl's and the EMT's. With a matching dislocated jaw, and the same pattern of torn-out flesh unfurling from where her mouth was supposed to be.

"They *are* all connected."

"What?" PJ called.

"Let's go. And don't look at the body."

James let his legs carry him down the stairs as he compared all of the victims. Minus the bullet wounds, the damage to their bodies was almost identical. The swarm he and Alek had run into in the stairwell was exactly like what he'd seen on the surveillance tape. And, assuming each of them had been taken over by the red cloud creature, it would explain why he and Schilling hadn't seen any obvious signs that there was someone else in Tyson's house at the time of his and his wife's deaths. "This is insane, but all of it's connected. I need to get to Eva."

"All of what's connected?" PJ panted as he reached the bottom of the stairs.

"Nothing. It's not important." He followed PJ out the door and into the narrow alley behind the hospital. "Thanks for helping me get out of there. I really appreciate it, but I've got to get back to the station. I'm sure it's a mess with all of this going on."

PJ put his hands on his thighs and sucked in air. "And what am I supposed to do?"

"Go home. And keep quiet about what happened in there. Just give it time. It'll all blow over."

"Hold up." PJ righted himself and planted his hands on his hips. "You want me to go back to my apartment and, what, pretend like none of this went down? Were we even in the same place? This isn't one of those take-some-time-off-and-it'll-get-better situations. This is clearly the beginning of something huge. We need to call Max Brooks or someone. The zombie apocalypse is upon us."

"PJ, those were not zombies. There is no apocalypse. You can go home. Everything is going to be fine," James said, unsure whether or not he was lying.

PJ frowned. "I'll trust you, but you are *not* getting rid of me. No way. No how. I'm small and weak, the perfect target. My best chance of survival is sticking with you."

"Fine. I really don't have time to argue with you right now, but you're on your own as soon as we get to the station."

"Deal."

James shook PJ's extended hand before turning and looking up at the hospital. "C'mon Alek. I don't trust you, but it looks like I might need you."

SEVENTEEN

The three frenzied men bucked and strained against Alek as he drove them down the hall. He let out a final, roaring grunt and tossed the snarling creatures backward. They slammed against a closed door at the end of the hall, and it splintered in half. Slivers of wood sprayed into the air and grazed Alek's skin as he raced into the room after them.

All three were on their feet, seemingly unaware of and unaffected by the brutal collision. One charged Alek, his arms flailing, spittle flying from his mouth. The immortal jumped to the side, grabbing the doctor's lab coat as he passed. Alek used the man's speed to propel him through the doorway and out into the hall.

He turned to the other two and gritted his teeth. "Who's next?" They rushed him simultaneously, and Alek unleashed his boxing skills. Combating the men wasn't difficult for the warrior. If all evil fought like these two, the Mortal Realm would have nothing to fear. No, striking them wasn't the hard part. However, achieving the desired result seemed more and more impossible. Alek fired a punch at the taller of the two for the fifth or sixth time in a row. He'd lost count by now. The whites of the man's eyes were red from broken capillaries, and chunks of flesh blew off his face with each increasingly violent strike. But he continued to push forward.

The other man was at his back, tearing at his shirt and howling like a wild beast. Alek bent his knees, reached over his shoulder for the doctor's arm, and flung him over his back to the ground. Air hissed out of his lungs as he smacked against the floor. With his grip still firmly around the man's wrist, Alek stomped on his shoulder and used both of his hands to twist the doctor's arm. Bones popped and tore through the flesh, but the man still hungrily clawed the air, trying to get to the immortal.

"I will finish you," Alek seethed. He picked up a shard of the broken door and drove it through the man's eye until it came to a sudden stop against the back of his skull. Finally, he went limp, but only for a moment. His body flopped vigorously on the tile. Blood splashed up from the steadily increasing puddle around his head.

"Red mist." For a moment, panic sprouted in his chest. He knew the flying creature would chase him, and he couldn't risk using a huge portion of his energy to run. Until he made contact with the Oracle, he had to stay in the Mortal Realm, and he wouldn't let this trip end like the last.

A suffocating gurgle echoed up from the floor, and the remaining man uttered a piercing screech and cowered in the corner, as if he knew what happened next. The swarm sprayed tissue and blood as it rushed from the corpse's mouth like water from a fountain. Alek grabbed the only other soul in the room and pushed him into the pulsing cloud. It split and went around the body, rocketing straight toward Alek. The noise it emitted was unlike anything he'd heard before. Its steady purr was not only audible—he also felt its constant thrumming like an itch under his skin.

We see you. The oily words slipped into his ears. *There is no escape.*

Alek stiffened. "Try if you must, but I will defeat you."

Humans. Always constructing promises you cannot keep. The scarlet specks rippled to a stop inches away from Alek. *Why do you not fear us, mortal?*

A smirk cracked Alek's lips. "I am no mortal. Try me. You will fail."

Lies, the swarm shrieked, and rushed its prey.

Smiling grimly, Alek did not struggle as they flooded his mouth and clouded his lungs.

EIGHTEEN

The tips of Eva's fingers throbbed from digging into the sides of the cardboard box all the way back to Bridget's car. At her house, the books hadn't seemed so heavy, but four blocks later her arms were burning, and her brisk stride had morphed into a steady shuffle. "I hope the next power I get is the ability to fly. Or super strength. I'd be good with that too."

Finally at the car, she dropped the box onto the pavement and collapsed against the popped trunk. The trunk light bathed the four hefty, worn books in a yellow glow as they stared up at Eva from the pinstriped lining.

"Now, which of you is the one filled with those scary stories? I guess I should say facts. Which of you is filled with scary facts?" She stared up at the starless sky and flipped through her childhood memories. Being a young girl, sneaking around her grandmother's house, looking for treasures while Yiayiá worked in the kitchen. The books had been stacked on top of her grandmother's bookshelf.

There were tons of colorful *tchotchkes* she could have easily played with, but the books seemed to whisper promises of adventure. They had found her more than she had found them. She'd push a chair up against the shelves, and brush her fingers along each cracked spine before choosing one to explore. Through the books she learned about Alastor and so many other creatures she believed existed only in nightmares.

Alastor.

The thought guided her toward memories she wasn't yet ready to face. The fetid stench of his breath, the slurps and pops as he'd torn the flesh from his form, his strong hand around her throat.

"Enough!" she shouted into the dark. "I don't have to think about that anymore." She took a deep breath and yanked down the sleeve of her jacket to cover the garish tattoo he'd branded her with. "They were in the same book, Alastor and the picture. They had to have been. It was the only one I took from the shelf." The covers stared up at her. Each had a different design branded into the flaking leather. She remembered the weight of the book as it lay open in her lap, and how she would trace the delicate pattern on the cover, admiring the beautiful simplicity of the design. "It's this one." She picked up the book and did what she'd done as a girl, and let her fingers wander the image. The slender handle of the inverted torch stretched down the center of the cover, flames licking its bottom edge.

Footsteps pounded the street behind her, and Eva clutched the book against her chest, ready to flee.

"It's just me," Bridget puffed. "Lord, why do people run?" She put her hands on her knees. "I hope you found what you were looking for, because that was not fun, and I broke my nail all the way down to the skin. It's bleeding and everything." She held her finger up for Eva to inspect.

"I definitely found what I need. Maybe now we'll get some answers." Eva piled the three remaining hardbacks in the box and closed the trunk.

"Aren't you going to at least try to heal my finger?"

"Bridget, we've been over this. I don't have any new abilities yet."

"But this wouldn't be a *new* ability, just an extension of one you already have."

"Fine. Let me see your finger." Bridget placed her injured digit on Eva's palm, and Eva wrapped her fingers around the bleeding mess. She stared at her fist, focusing on channeling her power through her hand and into Bridget's. "Is it working?"

"No, it just hurts because you're squeezing my bloody stump."

Eva dropped Bridget's hand and dug in her pocket for the car keys. "Well, I tried."

"Guess you can only heal yourself. Gah, you're so selfish." Bridget smiled. "But I do hope you figure it out before something really bad happens. Not that many things are worse than completely fucking up a totally good manicure." She started the car and maneuvered out of the tight parking space. "So, what did you find?"

The metallic image sparkled under the amber glow of the streetlights. "I don't know yet. I haven't had a chance to look through it, but from what I remember, it should tell us what we're dealing with."

"I get that you're going to use it to find out what kind of

monster thing is popping out of people's faces. What I don't get is what the book actually is. If I went into a store, where would I find that? I'm guessing on the big-ol'-boring-book clearance rack."

"It's not boring. At least, it wasn't when I looked at it years ago." She opened the book and thumbed through the first few pages. "It's like an encyclopedia."

"Oh, gag. I thought you said it wasn't boring, and that's the first word I think of when I hear encyclopedia."

"This isn't the Britannica kind of encyclopedia. This one is full of Greek legends and monsters."

"So you're in there then?"

"Very funny. I'm not a monster."

"That's not what I meant. Being an Oracle, that's totally part of the whole Greek legend thing. So shouldn't there be stuff in there about how you are what you are?"

"I don't know. I hadn't even thought about it."

"And people say I'm not smart." Bridget stomped on the gas and bolted into traffic. "Can you imagine how much easier all of this would've been if they'd just had the Internet back then? I'm sure all those stinky encyclopedias would be neatly categorized and available on some super-secret, Oracle-only website. One simple search, and we would've been done. But then again, I guess I wouldn't have gotten to improve my acting skills."

Eva switched on the overhead light and let Bridget's rambling dissolve into the background while she flipped through the book. Faded images of bloody scenes and frightening creatures covered the worn pages. "Oh my God. I found it. I found the picture."

Blue and red flashing lights coated the inside of the car,

and Eva's heart beat wildly within her chest.

"There must be some crazy shit going down at the hospital. I've never seen this many cops out at once." Bridget pulled over and waited for them to pass. "Now, what were you saying? You found the picture of the stuff that flew out of that dead guy's mouth in the video?"

Fear trapped the words in her throat, and she could only nod.

The police cruisers passed, and Bridget accelerated into traffic. "Well don't just sit there. Tell me what it says."

Eva silently read the short sentences accompanying the image. "If what this says is true, we're in a lot of trouble."

Nineteen

James had to call Bridget. She needed all of the facts for when Eva returned, and, since Alek was back, he assumed the Oracle wouldn't be far behind. He patted the pockets of his khakis in search of his cell. "Shit. My phone is in my car."

"I have mine," PJ said, offering it to James.

"No, I don't know her number. It's in my phone."

"Need to call your girlfriend to make sure she's hasn't been attacked by the non-zombies?" PJ asked.

"She's not my girlfriend, and we don't know if that stuff has even gotten out of the hospital. I'm sure it's being contained."

"Viruses, parasites, bacteria—none of them are ever truly contained or eliminated. That's just something the powers that be tell the general public to make them feel better."

"And for good reason. We don't want people freaking out over nothing," James murmured.

"Hey! You two can't be back here." A uniformed officer shone his flashlight at them, momentarily blinding James.

"It's okay." James shielded his eyes and pulled out his badge for the officer. "Doing a quick perimeter sweep, and I found this guy wandering around out here."

The officer studied the badge before handing it back. "If it makes it easier, I can get him out of your hair for you."

James paused and contemplated pawning PJ off on the officer. "I got it. I was finishing up anyway. Any word on what's going on in there?"

The officer switched off his flashlight and shook his head. "Haven't heard anything, but they do just have me walking in the same square around the building. Ask one of the guys outside the ER. They'll probably be able to tell you a lot more than me."

"That works. My car is parked there, so I'm headed that way now. We'll load up then drive to the station."

"I don't think that's going to work out for you. They might share some info, but they're not going to let you take your car. They've got the scene buttoned up pretty tight. You're going to have to hitch a ride with one of the cruisers that's been cleared for reentry."

"I'll do that. Thanks for your help. Stay safe tonight." James shook the officer's hand. "Shit!" he grumbled when they were far enough away.

"What is it?" PJ jogged to keep up with James's brisk stride.

"I need my car."

"Not really. He said we can get a ride back with one of the other cops." PJ reminded him.

"I don't want a ride back to the station, at least not yet. There's somewhere I need to go first."

PJ beamed. "Then it's a good thing you're with me. I happen to have a vehicle not far from here. Bet that makes you feel bad for thinking about giving me away to that other cop."

"It doesn't, but you'll let me use your car, no questions asked?"

"I'll let you use my *vehicle* question-free, but only if you take me with you. And you should feel bad, even if it's just a little bit."

"I don't. Now, take me to your car. We need to get there quick," James instructed.

They reached the end of the alley, and PJ took the first left, leading James away from the hospital. "There is one little thing I should probably tell you about my vehicle." He slowed to a stop in the driveway of a charming brick bungalow. He punched in a code on the garage keypad, and the door rose creakily.

"That's your car?" James pointed to the slick Lexus coupe resting in the uncluttered space.

"No, that's my boyfriend's. Mine is that one. The more eco-friendly vehicle." PJ smiled.

"PJ, that's not even a car."

"To be fair, I never said it was. I said it's a vehicle, which isn't a lie."

"Just give me the keys and get on."

James rounded the dingy, paint-chipped moped and sat on the cracked leather seat.

"There's an extra helmet in the compartment on the back." PJ snapped his own helmet in place and wrapped his arms around James's middle.

James shook his head and keyed the buzzing engine. "I should have stayed in Texas."

• • •

Alek's eyelids squeezed shut when the swarm rushed toward him, filling his mouth and burning his chest as they bore into his lungs. It felt like the air had been sucked out of the room, and he dizzily groped for something to steady his shaking body. The buzzing in his ears intensified, throwing him even more off balance. The room seemed to spin, and Alek flapped his arms to keep from falling. Glass shattered around him, and empty air met his back. His hands grazed fabric, and he gripped it for stability, but it only followed him out the window.

The fall took only seconds, but felt like an eternity as he flailed in the air, trying to force his feet under him. His body wouldn't listen to the commands his blurred thoughts struggled to convey, and he crashed into the pavement. The concrete fractured beneath him, and pain spider webbed through his torso, making every breath excruciating. The pain was made worse by the body wriggling on top of him. The buzz faded to a low hum, allowing Alek to gain control of his movements. He unclenched his hands from the doctor's coat and pushed the twitching man to the side. He rubbed his palm across his chest and coughed to ease the tingling building in the back of his throat. With each forceful hack, red specks flew from his mouth and dotted the pavement.

You are strong. We need more like you—powerful. The disembodied voice whirred between his ears. *A carrier able to withstand infection.*

"Infection?" His throat ached.

A cleanse. Wiping each corrupt realm so it may start anew under Her control. They rooted around in his thoughts, forcing memories forward and creating a dull ache in his head. *So much potential within you. For great things. Dark things.*

"*Call me H. So, do we have a deal?*" The memory was distant and cold, vanishing before he could probe it further.

What class of human are you?

Alek gathered his bearings and pushed himself off the ground. "I am no mortal."

Pieces of the Underworld flow within your veins, but the gods have long been absent from this realm.

"I am no god." Alek wiped at the dried blood covering his healed knuckles as he shuffled to finish off the doctor, who was clawing at the pavement, determined to reach him.

You are one of the immortals! They shrieked the words with such force that Alek dropped to his knees. *Your kind deceived us before.* Pressure mounted in his lungs, and the deafening buzz returned. *Never again,* they screeched, and tore out of his mouth. The muscles in Alek's jaw stretched to capacity and fought against the swarm's need to make more room. Heat rippled through his chest and poured into his mouth as the last of the flecks joined the palpitating cloud hovering over the slithering doctor. *Never again,* they repeated, before diving past the man's lips.

Unable to stand, Alek took shallow breaths through the pain while the man in the soiled coat rose to his feet. Flaps of flesh fell from his face and splatted against the road as he stood. *It will do no good to remain here, immortal.* The voice of the creature inside the doctor merged with his, forming one echoing baritone. *Return to the Underworld. This realm is ours.*

Through his blurred vision, Alek watched the creature in the broken body sprint out of the alleyway. Alek reached for his talisman and clenched it between his fingers. "The Oracle. Take me to the Oracle."

TWENTY

"What do you mean, Eva? In a lot of trouble how?" The car swerved as Bridget craned her neck to see what was on the page.

"Bridge, concentrate on driving. None of this matters if they're scraping us off the side of the road." The book bounced in Eva's lap as Bridget maneuvered the car along the uneven street.

"You can't just tell me we're in a lot of trouble and then not explain why. Tell me."

"First we need to get back to your place, so I can get in contact with Tartarus. This book has some info in it, some scary info, but not enough. And if even this little bit is true, we'll for sure need help." Eva studied the frightening drawing. The colors were faded, and age had worn the image, but it was exactly as Eva remembered. A man on his back, his face mangled and distorted, a cloud of scarlet specks hovering above him.

"So, we need Alek's moms to help us?" Bridget asked.

"Yes, but more importantly, we need Alek."

"Amen, sister. I've been wondering when that sweet hunk of eye candy was going to appear back in this, what are they calling it? Universe? Timeline?"

"Realm," Eva said.

"Yeah, this realm could definitely use a little bit more Alek. You excited to have him back?" Bridget asked.

Eva's cheeks warmed. "I am, actually. He saved my life."

"Again? Gah, this guy is totally on a mission. And you didn't even tell me about it. You said that his mom pulled you out of this realm and into Tartarus. How long were you going to hold out on me? Spill. I want all the details."

"I mean, I guess *he* didn't really save my life." Eva's chest tingled as she told the story. "I wasn't actually going to die, but he was. He would have died for me. Just to make sure I was safe."

"Oh, swoon. If that doesn't deserve a visit from Miss Kitty, I don't know what does." Bridget pulled up to the parking garage and waved her keycard in front of the detector.

"I barely know him. I don't even know what his last name is, or if he has one. But I wouldn't have sex with him even if he'd been around for months and months, and I knew everything about him. We work together, and it would make things weird."

"Having not ever been a part of an office romance, I would have no idea, but I feel like hooking up with a coworker would be exciting. The whole forbidden-fruit aspect really gets me. I wonder if the store will be hiring any guys soon. I should write that down and put it in our comments box." Bridget swung the car into her parking space and turned off the ignition. "Anyway, you should never say never."

"I didn't say never."

"No, but you implied it, and that's what matters. Well, that and finding out what kind of heat your warrior boy is packing." She winked and hopped out of the car. "Just surrender to the insta-love, Eva. You're in it already, even if you don't realize it."

Eva hunched her shoulders, pulled the cap down over her eyebrows, and zipped the book up in her jacket. "Insta-love?" she grunted, as she struggled to keep the weighty hardback clutched against her stomach.

Bridget paused to admire her manicure before punching the elevator button. "You know, girl meets boy and there are sparks right from the get-go. Think Romeo and Juliet."

Relief washed over Eva when the doors opened, revealing an empty metal box. "But Romeo and Juliet were practically children."

"You're never too young or too old for the magical powers of insta-love. Plus, it's almost like you have a kid together. Like this realm is your baby, and you're attached until it grows up and isn't evil anymore." Bridget grinned and tapped the button for her floor. "Eva, relax a smidge. No one knows you're here, and I'm pretty sure that, even if they did, they wouldn't want that old book."

The elevator doors opened, and Bridget stepped out into the hallway. "All clear," she said, motioning for Eva to follow. They hurried to Bridget's front door, where she stopped to type in her lock code. "It feels kind of like we're spies or something, doesn't it?" She giggled and pushed open the door.

"I don't know. I guess so."

"Come on, Eva. Have a little bit of fun with this. You're literally the only person on the planet who's experiencing all this right now. Just take a frickin' second to enjoy the greatness that is you and your Oraclehood. It's pretty badass if you think about it."

"You know what? You're right." Eva leaned her hips against the dining room table and slowly unzipped her jacket. The heavy hardback hit the wood with a slap.

"Well, of course I am."

"There's no point in being so stressed about something I can't change."

"Why would you want to change it? I know it's brought you a lot of shit, but you have something some people would kill to have. You're a completely unique individual in a culture that wants nothing more than to smash us into clichéd little groups."

"Wow, Bridge, that's actually really insightful."

"Just because society has put me in the dumb, slutty blonde category doesn't mean I'm not really a smart, slutty blonde."

Eva flipped the book open to the page she'd earmarked.

"That has to be the same stuff, right?" Bridget peered over Eva's shoulder.

"I'm pretty sure. I mean, it looks the same, but that's why we're calling Tartarus."

"You said that this book said we're in trouble. The picture is creepy, and I definitely get that it looks the same as what we saw in the video, but I don't see anything that says we need to freak out and run for the hills."

"You can't just look at the picture. You have to read what they wrote about it."

"I would, but there aren't any words on the page."

Eva glanced down at the paper, then back up at Bridget. "They're right there." She pointed to the few sentences she'd read and reread in the car. "It says, 'Breathe in this creature, and perish. Bearer of disease and plague. No mortal will survive the Nosoi.' I'm probably not pronouncing it correctly."

"You're just messing with me, right? I don't see any words on the page. Only this mildly disgusting picture and those weird design things up in the corner." Bridget nodded toward the sentences Eva had just read aloud.

"Those weird design things are what some of us call letters. I know you're not a big reader, but you sure as hell know what words look like."

"Those aren't any letters I've seen before. Let's just call Tartarus. Maybe someone there will be able to explain why you've suddenly gone crazier than usual."

Eva rolled her eyes and pulled the gold chain out from under her shirt. She unclasped it and let the vial of water slide into her hand.

"Need a bowl or something?" Bridget asked.

Eva shrugged. "I guess so. In Tartarus this water is kept in a big, pretty birdbath-looking thing, but they do have way more of it."

"Well, this should work. It *is* water anyway, and water is water is water." Bridget set down a small bowl.

The tiny bottle cooled Eva's palm as she wrapped her fingers around it and removed the cork. "Well, here we go." She poured out the beryl blue water, and stared into the bowl.

"Now what? Is a keypad going to pop up so you can

dial?" Bridget asked.

"Maiden said all I have to do is put my fingers in the water and think of Tartarus."

"So, what are you waiting for? Let's get this show on the road," Bridget cheered.

"I don't know. I'm nervous all of a sudden."

"Oh please, the man pretty much died trying to protect you. I'm sure he won't care that you have horribly flat hat hair."

Electricity popped, and an initially tame breeze rolled into forceful gusts, tangling Eva's hair and sending fear snaking down her spine.

"What's happening?" Bridget's words were swept up in the wind.

"I don't know!" Eva tried to shout back over the crackling roar.

The air settled as a shape took form.

"Alek?" Eva breathed.

Sweat glistened off his bare arms and the sculpted muscles of his chest and abs played peekaboo through the rips in his shirt. The corner of Eva's mouth curled into a lascivious half smile.

Bridget leaned into her and whispered, "Insta-love."

"Eva," Alek gasped, before falling into one of the zebra-striped chairs.

Eva rushed to his side. "Are you okay?"

"I only need a moment to recover." He took a few deep breaths, and the color returned to his cheeks. "Have you been in contact with Tartarus?" He wasted no time getting down to business.

"I was just about to call. I thought you were waiting to

hear from me before you came here."

"Hang on," Bridget interrupted. "What happened to saying hi to people when you materialize uninvited in the middle of their living room? It's pretty impressive how totally spot on you are with your landings, by the way."

"Yes, I know." Alek cleared his throat. "But there isn't time for that. Something went wrong. I had to come to the Mortal Realm sooner than planned."

"What happened? Are your mothers okay?" Eva asked. "Are you okay? You look like you've been fighting."

"Considering what happened, I'm fine, and for now Tartarus remains the same. It is this realm I am worried for. An infection is spreading. It's alive and it does not belong with mortals."

"An infection?" Eva carried the book to Alek and pointed to the picture. "Does it look something like this?"

"That is exactly what we saw."

"We? Who's we? Isn't Eva the only one you're supposed to be teaming up with?" Bridget asked.

"The detective. Has he made it to you?"

Three quick knocks echoed from the direction of Bridget's front door.

"I'm going to just take a stab in the dark and say that that's him right now." She opened the door without looking through the peephole.

"We need to talk." James burst through the door. PJ trailed him and waved shyly at Bridget. She shot Eva a puzzled glance.

I have no idea, Eva mouthed back.

"You're alive." He looked at Alek, expressionless. "Good. Don't want your body muddying up an already complicated scene."

"Wait a second. What's going on here? I've only been gone for a day and you two are having sex, you guys are off fighting crime together, and there's some otherworldly infection attacking my city."

"I knew it!" PJ clapped.

"And who the hell is that?" Bridget asked.

Alek took a few steps toward the visitor and puffed out his chest. "Yes, my thought exactly. Who are you?"

"He's direct, right to the point. I like that in a man. Name's PJ. That's short for Patrick Johann. But, I can assure you, it's the only thing short about me." He extended his hand to Alek, and his cheeks flushed pink. "Sorry, that was not my best line."

Alek turned to face James. "Why did you bring him?"

"It's a long story. We have more important things to talk about," James said.

"Yeah, but how are we going to do that with this new guy lurking in the background? No offense." Bridget offered PJ a polite smile.

"James, Bridget's right. Bringing him here was a really bad decision, and we don't have time for those. No offense, PJ, but now is not the time to make new friends." She grinned and waved at him cordially.

"PJ." Alek plopped a broad hand on his shoulder, and he wobbled. "Has anyone ever struck you in the face before?"

PJ's eyes widened as Alek's fist made contact with his cheek. Instantly his legs buckled, and he crumpled to the floor.

"Jesus Christ, Alek!" Eva rushed to PJ and gently tucked his bangs behind his ear to survey the damage.

"He's out cold."

"Our PJ problem has been resolved. You are welcome." He shook his shaggy mane from his eyes and smiled broadly.

"At least help me get him to the couch," Eva instructed.

Effortlessly, Alek scooped him off the floor and dropped him onto the sofa.

"Now, can we just take a minute to figure out what's going on?" Eva asked.

"We only had sex the one time. Well, two if we're being specific," Bridget said.

"That's so not what I'm talking about."

"Oh." She crossed her arms and sunk onto the couch next to PJ.

"We made contact at the hospital," Alek began.

"Where we saw some crazy shit you're not going to believe. Actually, I forgot where I'm at; you're definitely going to believe it," James added.

"We encountered the creature you showed me. The one from the book," Alek said.

"The Nosoi?"

Alek nodded. "My mothers spoke of this evil, but they said there is no way the Nosoi could be in this realm. It's jailed in Tartarus."

"I hate to say this, but they're probably wrong. All the evidence points to the Nosoi being here, now." Eva marched to the dining room table and stared at her reflection in the bowl of water. "We have to find out what the Furies know."

TWENTY-ONE

Sabrina Masten walked into the Brook Restaurant and Bar, and swept her gaze around the room until she saw her friend waving enthusiastically from a table across the way. She hurried to her, hung her purse on the back of the high-backed barstool, and collapsed onto its cushy seat. "Sorry I'm late. Traffic was horrible. A bunch of roads are closed off, and I had to go about five miles out of the way to get here."

"No problem. Breanna and Whitney have texted me pretty much that same exact sentence already."

"You work for the city's planning department. What kind of never-ending construction are they starting now?" Sabrina asked.

"There isn't anything new scheduled for this area, but they did just say the cops have blocked off a big section around the hospital." She pointed to one of the many TVs hanging around the bar.

"Hmm, weird. Hopefully they'll have gotten their shit

together by the time we leave." Sabrina caught the bartender's eye and motioned for him to come over. "I'll have one of whatever she's having, and bring us each a shot of Fireball."

"Fireball, wow. I don't know if I'm up for it. Work that bad, huh?"

"Aubrey, you have no idea. They're restructuring things, which is just a nice way of saying that they've fired a bunch of people. Not only does it not make any sense, but they've also not bothered to do anything about the workload. I'm doing myself what, just last week, I shared with four other people. It's a big fuck you to everyone left."

"Why don't you just quit?"

"Right, and work where? I have a business degree from a crappy state school just like 80 percent of the people our age. I don't want to be out of work and living back home with my parents. I should probably be happy I have a career at all." She raised her shot glass and her smile widened. "I want to stumble out of here, and preferably not alone."

"Cheers to that!" Aubrey clinked her glass against Sabrina's, and the women downed their shots. "How long has it been anyway?"

"How long has what been?"

"You know exactly what I'm talking about. You broke up with that asshole Anthony over four months ago, and I haven't heard you talk about anyone else. I'm not saying you need to date someone, just, you know, maybe spread the love a little bit." Aubrey laughed and waved her hand over Sabrina's crossed legs.

"I know. I know. Believe me, I am more than over this dry spell. I'll make sure tonight's the night." She smiled and cast her gaze around the sparsely populated room.

"So, what happened with that guy you met on Match.com? Bryan, right?"

"Close. This one's name is Ryan, but I don't know if I'm going to keep him around."

"Why? Did he order four shots of Patrón and get hammered in the first twenty minutes like the last guy you met up with?" Sabrina laughed.

"Oh, don't remind me. He was so sloppy. I'm trying to block that encounter from my memory."

Sabrina laughed and took a sip of her Chardonnay.

"Oh, shit." Aubrey stared over Sabrina's shoulder, her eyes wide. "Speaking of encounters you want to block."

"No fucking way," Sabrina groaned. "God, this city is way too small."

"Brina!" Anthony bellowed, and stumbled over.

Cigarettes and beer assaulted her nostrils, and she craned her neck away from the stench. "Don't call me that."

"What, you never had a problem with it when we were together." His heavy arm slithered across her shoulders as he ordered a drink from the bartender.

"Yeah, but we're not together anymore, Anthony." She shrugged his arm off of her back.

"And whose fault is that?"

"Yours, you fucking skeeze," Aubrey interjected. "Now go away. It's obvious no one wants you here."

"Thanks, Aubrey, but I'll leave as soon as Brina tells me to go. And, so far, it looks like she wants me to stay."

"Leave, Anthony," Sabrina said without missing a beat.

"C'mon, Sabrina. You know I'm sorry." He picked up the bottle of beer he'd ordered and took a long swig. "Fine. I can take a hint. Gonna go hit the head, but I'll be around for awhile in case you realize."

"In case I realize what?"

"In case you realize," he repeated wistfully. He lifted her hand, and gave it a quick kiss before shuffling off to the bathroom.

Aubrey cringed. "Ugh, he's so disgusting."

"Tell me about it." Sabrina used a cocktail napkin to wipe off the back of her hand.

"I have no idea what you saw in him. You can do so much better."

"Yeah. Thanks Aubrey." Sabrina's stomach knotted. "I, uh—I'm not feeling so hot. I think I'm going to head out."

"What? You never go out, and you just got here. Don't let that asshole ruin your night."

"No, it's not because of Anthony," she lied. "I just have to be up early, so I really need to get home." Sabrina stood, dug her wallet out of her purse, and waved her credit card at the bartender.

"At least stay with me until one of the other girls get here," Aubrey whined.

"Ugh. Fine." She set her card on the bar top and flopped back into the chair. "But I'm leaving the second one of them shows."

The door chimed as more patrons entered the bar.

"Maybe they're here!" Aubrey stood on her tiptoes and peered at the front door. "Oh, gross." Her face wrinkled like she'd just gotten a whiff of something rotten.

"Who is it now? I don't think I can handle another ex." Sabrina craned her neck to check out who'd arrived.

A man dressed in a remarkably convincing zombie costume shuffled into the bar, growling and twitching like a feral animal.

The bartender stepped out from behind the bar, blocking him from coming in any further. "Hey, man. We're kind of far out from Halloween." The bar went silent.

The man bared his teeth and growled ferociously.

"Oh, yeah, I'm really scared. If it was up to me, you could stay. I'd even give you a free shot for the killer makeup job, but I need this gig, so you're going to have to leave and come back." The bartender grabbed the towel hanging from his back pocket and wiped off his hands. "I'll have a beer waiting for you after you go get cleaned up."

Sabrina leaned into Aubrey. "Just wait, the punch line will come any minute now."

• • •

A shrill squeal permeated the bathroom, electrifying the hairs on the back of Anthony's neck. He turned the faucet off and listened. Another scream, this time louder and more guttural. He wiped his hands on his jeans and charged into the bar. Shock sucked the air from his lungs, and he stumbled into the wall behind him.

A body lay in a heap at the front of the bar, its jaw unnaturally stretched away from its bleeding face. Fear and panic contorted the faces of the bar patrons as they hacked up red tinged mucus.

"Brina." Anthony shot through the sputtering crowd to where he'd last seen her. "Sabrina, are you alright?"

Her knuckles turned white as she clung to the bar top with one hand and gripped her wine glass with the other. Coughs racked her body, and she struggled to breathe.

"I'm freaking out. We need to go to the hospital."

Sabrina's wine glass shattered in her palm. A large sliver protruded from her skin, and she yanked it out of the oozing wound. "Prepare. The queen is coming."

Silence coated the bar as each person turned to face him. They spoke with hushed reverence, red dripping from their lips. "The queen is coming! The queen is coming!"

Snarling, Sabrina sprang forward and slammed a shard of glass into his pectoral muscle.

"Ah, fuck!" He screamed and shoved her backward.

She stumbled and tripped over a barstool. Her head slapped against the countertop, and her body locked as she slid down the face of the bar, a crimson streak marking her descent.

Anthony pulled the glass from his chest and dropped it on the floor. "Brina?"

Her body bounced wildly, knocking her head against the wood with deep, repeating thuds.

Gurgling hisses sounded around Anthony as the group closed in on him. He snatched Sabrina's purse, cradled her against his body, and tore through the sea of bloodshot eyes and clawing hands. In the safety of the street, he studied Sabrina's face. Her eyelids were open slightly, but he could see only the whites of her eyes.

"Oh God, oh God. Brina, baby, stay with me. We're almost to the car."

He placed her gently on the concrete before pawing through her purse for her car keys. "I found them. I found them. Everything's going to be okay. You're going to be okay." He stared at her motionless form, and it hit him. Everything wasn't going to be okay. "I'm so sorry. For everything." Anguish sucked the strength from his legs, and he crumpled to the ground next to her body.

Her back arched again, and Anthony shuffled to the side to give her room. Blood bubbled from her mouth and poured onto the cement. A wet, choking noise emanated from her throat as her larynx bulged. Scarlet specks tore out of her mouth and shot into the night sky. The cloud rippled and pulsed in the air above him. He scrambled to his feet and smashed the key fob to unlock the car. The pulsating swarm rained down on the car as he darted into the safety of the vehicle.

They pelted the roof and zipped past the windshield, screeching as they disappeared into the night.

The queen is coming!

TWENTY-TWO

The hours of training in the dark caves of the Underworld, the handful of times he'd visited the Mortal Realm to return the escaped evil to its place in Tartarus, his battle with Alastor, all of it had readied Alek to face the next level of ancient villain, but, more than that, it had been what he craved. Until now. Now there was an emptiness within him. Something the hunger for battle and glory no longer filled.

The warrior within you is fading. Refuse him, let him die, and what creature will you be?

Pythia's words pressed against his thoughts, and Alek rolled the remaining half of his talisman between his fingers. He squeezed the sharp edge of the cracked crystal and let the pain drown out the specter's warning.

Eva waved her hand in front of his face. "Alek, are you going to help me with this or not?"

"Yes, of course," he responded, unsure of what he'd agreed to. "Help you with what?"

Eva put her hand on her hip and pointed to the bowl

of water on the dining room table. "We have to get in touch with your mothers, and this is really not the time to stop listening to me."

He grabbed her hand with both of his, and rubbed his thumbs in slow circles over her soft skin. "I'll do whatever you require."

"Oh, well." She took her hand off her hip and twirled the ends of her tousled hair. "For starters, I just need you to put your fingers in this water so we can call your home."

"I can think of something else she needs you to put your fingers in." Bridget winked.

"Thanks for that, Bridge. Now, we put our fingers in here and think of Tartarus, right?"

"Yes, you must focus your intention and think of nothing else."

"Okay." Eva closed her eyes and dipped her fingertips in the still water. "Tartarus, Tartarus, Tartarus."

Alek followed her lead and cleared his mind of all thoughts except those of his home in the Underworld. With his eyes closed, Tartarus morphed from its true dark and craggy form to the bright and restored realm he hoped the future would one day bring.

"Whoa, guys, doesn't that feel weird?" Bridget whispered.

A cyclone of water spun up from the bowl, lifting Alek's and Eva's hands inches from where they started. "I was unaware it was happening." He removed his fingers and felt warmth roll off Eva's arm as she shuffled closer to him.

"It's not going to suck us up, is it?" Bridget asked, hooking her arm through James's.

"No," Alek breathed. "It will only reveal my home to you."

A sharp trill rang out, and Alek waited, ears perked.

"Alek!" The water spun and contorted to form a perfect recreation of Maiden's face. A broad smile lifted the corner of her eyes and created a small dimple beneath the apple of her right cheek. "How are you? And you, Eva, you are looking much better than when you departed. It is excellent to hear from you and see you both together. I hope you are well."

"Temper your excitement, sister. This is a mission. Not a call to discuss pleasantries," Mother said flatly, her form rippling to life.

Alek stiffened his broad shoulders. "Mother, we have guests."

"Hi." Bridget smiled and waved enthusiastically.

"You must be Bridget." Maiden tucked a strand of hair behind her ear. "I have heard much about you."

"It's all true, I'm sure," Bridget said.

Maiden turned her attention to James. "And you, I have seen you before."

"Hi, I'm Detective Graham." He stepped forward and waved awkwardly.

"Ah, yes. The detective. Since both of you are here, I am sure you know the true purpose of Alek's presence in your realm."

"Yeah, we pretty much know it all, and we're here to help in any way we can," Bridget chimed in.

"*Almost* any way," James interjected. "I won't put people in any more danger than they're already in."

"If you have finished," Mother said sternly. "Alek, would you like to inform us why you have made contact?"

"Actually, calling you was my decision." Eva hesitated. "I, um—I don't really know how to say this, so I'll just say it.

I think that maybe the Nosoi are here."

"The Nosoi?" A ball of liquid shot out of the bowl and spun to reveal Crone.

"That cannot be true." Water sloshed back and forth as Maiden shook her head.

"Well, I could be wrong, but I saw a pretty convincing video of them leaving the host body. It also matches what I read in my grandmother's old book."

"And you think a mortal's old book contains true information about the Nosoi? No mortal would live after coming into contact with such a creature, much less pen their experience," Mother chuckled.

Alek's stomach clenched with growing embarrassment for his mother's abrasive personality.

"I get that it sounds crazy," Eva said, "but that's even what it says in the book. That no mortal will survive the Nosoi."

Alek stepped closer to the liquid figures before speaking. "Maiden, in the stories of the past you used to tell me when I was a child, did you not mention ancient books that were written as a catalogue of all the evil in the realms?"

"The Tomes," Maiden whispered. "The Tomes, sisters. She has the Tomes. She must. As you said, Mother, no mortal would live to tell of their experience with the Nosoi."

"But wait, that's not the only thing that sounds crazy," Bridget added. "There's not even anything written on the page. It's just a bunch of scratchy little designs."

"Your friend, she is unable to read the text?" Crone asked.

"She keeps telling me nothing's written on there, but I swear there is something."

"And you, Alek, are you able to read the passage?"

He reached in front of Eva and slid the book across the table and read the sentences aloud. "'Breathe in this creature, and perish. Bearer of disease and plague. No mortal will survive the Nosoi.'"

"That's exactly what I see too," Eva blurted.

"Maiden, you are correct. I thought they had been lost. Yet, she does possess the Tomes. There is no other explanation," Crone said.

"The Oracle and immortals are the only souls able to read from the Tomes," Maiden explained. "They will be of great use to you both. They contain more than just a catalogue of evils. You must keep them safe."

"If we're the only people who can read this, then why did my grandmother have them? She knew, didn't she?"

Alek gripped Eva's shaking shoulder, steadying her. "We each have our own destiny. Now you can be sure this is yours," he whispered.

"Right now, what your grandmother may have known is of no concern. We must concentrate on the task at hand. What are we to do about the Nosoi?" Mother asked.

"We know no mortal can survive after encountering this creature. We witnessed that first hand," Alek said, nodding toward James. "And written in the Tome is a warning that it's the bearer of disease and plague."

"Are we talking a hazmat suit type of epidemic here, or what?" James asked.

"The Nosoi were much more than carriers of pestilence," Crone explained. "They were an ancient creation used by the Gods to keep the realms in balance."

"Well, besides the pestilence part, they don't sound too horrible," Eva said.

"Yeah, they're just like weird little policemen," Bridget added.

"You have not seen what we have. They are brutal, relentless," Alek said.

"You are correct, my son. The swarm does not care about your existence. Over the millennia, they have evolved, become smarter and more ruthless. They have had time to study the mortal race and master the weapons needed to bring about its extermination," Mother said.

"Think of the deadly illnesses that have plagued humanity throughout time. All were created through infection by the Nosoi," Maiden added. "With each appearance made by the Nosoi, a new plague was born. This was all done in an attempt to cull your species."

"But power changes creatures, makes them hungry for more," Mother said.

"And now they desire this realm for their own," Alek rumbled.

"Why us? If they can go anywhere, why this realm?" Eva asked.

"Most creatures that escape Tartarus can sense you, Eva, and are drawn to you. After all, a member of your bloodline helped to put them there. They do not forget easily." Maiden turned her attention toward Bridget and James. "Each of your lives is forever changed because you are allied with the Oracle."

"Also, what enjoyment would they receive in doing away with a species lacking the intelligence to combat it?" Mother asked. "Mortals create vaccines and procedures to delay what eventually comes to you all. You are the only creatures who do so."

"James showed me the video," Bridget interjected, "and he didn't say anything about the victim having a plague. I'm sure the medical examiner would've recognized that right off the bat."

"Your science takes time, and, with enough of it, they will discover the infection," Maiden said.

"This is bad. This is really bad. What am I supposed to do when I get a call from the ME about this new disease?" James asked.

Alek's chest swelled with determination. "We won't let it get that far."

"Keep calm. There is more about the Nosoi you must know. In the beginning, as they are awakening from centuries of sleep and learning, the toxins they excrete will rapidly destroy the human body. In time, they will refine this deadly poison to create the perfect walking plague," Crone said.

Confusion twisted Eva's features. "I don't understand. So they escaped Tartarus to come here and turn us into their plague minions?"

"They have not escaped. Not completely. They are one of the few creatures requiring that their powers build before switching realms. They need to absorb energy from their victims to travel," Maiden said.

"And because they are interconnected, if a piece of the Nosoi remains in the Mortal Realm, it will only be a matter of time before they gather enough energy to supply the mass that is under our control. You must stop them before they are able to free themselves. For our realm and yours," Mother said.

"But you must be careful," Crone warned. "They are elusive beings, continually learning, adapting, and changing.

The more energy they absorb, the less time they will reside outside of a host. They will not want to expend their stored energy searching for a vessel."

Visions of how to defeat this foe eluded him, and Alek asked, "The piece that is jailed, how was it captured?"

"Yeah, is there a special weapon or vacuum thing that'll suck them up?" Bridget asked.

"They are greedy, and, given the opportunity, will search for strength within their victims. We were able to take advantage of that and lure them into the body of an immortal," Mother said.

Crone spoke. "You must get to them soon. They have been dormant for many decades. They will need time to relearn their skills and awaken their memories."

"Get to them before this happens, and you may have a chance of again tricking them," Maiden said.

"We have an immortal right here." James nodded toward Alek. "I knew you'd eventually be useful."

"That will not work this time. They already tried to infect me and realized what I am."

"If we can't use Alek, how are we supposed to defeat them?" Eva asked.

"The Nosoi are creatures of the air. They cannot survive buried in earth or drowned in water, and they will burn in fire," Crone said.

"So, just to clarify, since we can't get them to think Alek is a free buffet, we're supposed to somehow catch these crazy flying creatures, and put them in a box to burn them, bury them, or drown them?" Eva asked.

"That is why you must make haste," Crone said.

Frustrated with having wasted their only advantage,

Alek crossed his arms over his chest and huffed. "How are we to find them?"

"They are still in the early stages of relearning their skills. If not, those that are jailed here would already be free. Their victims will display madness and illness, both symptoms of the pestilence they favor," Crone explained.

Bridget threw her hands into the air. "Well that's going to be a bunch of people. I can probably walk down the street and find someone with a snotty nose who seems crazy."

Eva nodded. "I'm with Bridget on this one. Those two things are really vague."

"This sickness is different, obvious," James said.

"And those who escaped from the hospital fled on foot. They can't be far," Alek said.

"You let some of those infected things get away? I thought you were Mister Kill-everything-evil-that-moves," Bridget chided.

Alek clenched his teeth and calmed his anger before speaking. "My job is not always as simple as you might think."

"He did save my ass." James stared at Alek; his temples pulsed as he chewed on an imaginary wad of gum. "If it wasn't for him, I'd probably be one of those possessed things right now."

"Our son is a great warrior, but he will need your help if he is to defeat the Nosoi," Maiden said.

James grunted unintelligibly.

"We're here for him." Eva leaned against Alek's arm and intertwined her fingers with his. Warmth tingled up from his hand and lifted the corners of his mouth.

"Be careful, my son. Do not make the same foolish mistake that almost ended you last time," Mother warned.

"Sacrificing myself for the safety of the Oracle is something I will always be prepared to do." He gently squeezed Eva's hand.

"It is part of his duty," Maiden added.

"Becoming emotional is not a part of a warrior's duty," Mother seethed.

"Sister, you have stewed in your melancholy for decades. Open your eyes. Why would you wish that on our son?" Without waiting for a response, Maiden gathered her skirts and backed away, her watery figure splashing back onto the table.

Crone cleared her throat. "We will be going. Make haste, and remember to return home when you grow weary."

The room fell silent as the figures of the two remaining Furies burst apart and rained onto the table.

Twenty-Three

Discomfort rested heavy in the air, and James squirmed under its oppressive shroud. "I have to get back to the station and act like none of this is happening."

If he'd been thinking about turning away from the massive amount of crazy he'd unknowingly walked into, the look on Eva's face would have made him reconsider. "After everything you just heard, you're not going to help us?"

"Of course I'm going to help, but the best way for me to do that is to go back, do my job, and make sure no one finds out about what's really going on."

"Isn't it great having a man on the inside?" Bridget mused.

PJ groaned from the couch.

"Shit, I almost forgot about him." James carefully helped PJ into a seated position. "Hey, man. You slipped when we walked in. Took a hard fall and knocked yourself out. How are you feeling?"

"Confused," PJ croaked, rubbing at the bruise forming

on his jaw line. "Didn't that guy hit me? And weren't they talking about an alien disease?"

"What? No."

"Yeah, this guy's just a big ol' teddy bear." Eva wrapped her arm around Alek and squeezed. "He'd never hurt anyone."

"Right, and there are no alien diseases from the Underworld. None at all. Absolutely zero." A wide grin stretched across Bridget's face.

James darted a quick, disapproving glance at Bridget. "But we should be leaving. I have to find my partner and get you to the station, right Peej?"

PJ blinked groggily at James. "Peej?"

"Yeah, that—that didn't work out so well." James draped PJ's arm around his shoulder and hefted him to his feet. "I'll keep in touch with you guys and let you know what's happening on my end."

Bridget rushed to the front door ahead of James and PJ and opened it so they could hobble out. "We're still going on that date after this is all over." The corners of her hazel eyes lifted with her smile.

"Of course. I'm looking forward to it." He smiled back, unsure whether or not he was lying.

James helped PJ into the elevator and, when they finally shuffled out of the building, propped him against a light post in the condo's visitor parking lot.

"Your friends are a little strange." PJ winced as he fastened the chin strap on his helmet.

"Yeah, they are my friends," he said, more to himself than to PJ. "And they're definitely strange." Happiness warmed James's chest, and he smiled to himself. He hadn't thought he would ever get that feeling back, not without Mel. But there he was, on a scooter in downtown Tulsa, a plague from Hell floating through the city, and James Graham was the happiest he'd been in a year.

• • •

Eva sank into the couch and threw her feet onto the coffee table. "That was a lot more intense than I expected."

"The Nosoi are formidable opponents," Alek said, plopping down next to her.

"And I have no idea how we're going to defeat them. I'm still a little confused about that part." She stretched her arms overhead and yawned.

"How about this. I'll go down to my car and get that box of books from the trunk. The Furies did say the books would be able to help us."

"Good idea, Bridge." Eva hefted herself off the couch. "I'll come with."

She shook her head. "Nah, you stay. I need a little breather. Hearing about all this stuff has got me kind of stressed." She grabbed her keys and flitted out the door.

Eva shuffled back to the couch and collapsed next to Alek. Awkward silence hovered around them, and Eva blurted the first comment that came to mind. "So, Mother, she's kind of tough. I get the feeling she does *not* like me."

"I must apologize if she made you feel that way. I am certain it's not about you. The issue goes much deeper than we know."

"I can't say that makes me feel that any better, but thank you." She rested her hand on his and let her fingers trace his thick callouses. "Bridget said that we're suffering from insta-love. Isn't that funny? Like you and I have real feelings for each other." Her gaze met his, and he stared at her so intently that she felt her cheeks get hot. "Why are you—"

Before she could complete her thought, Alek was pressed against her. The heat from his body brought goose bumps to her skin. He slipped his hand into her hair and gripped the base of her neck, pulling her closer. Her body pulsed as his kiss deepened and became more forceful. She wrapped her arms around his broad back and traced the ripples of his muscles under the fabric. She moaned softly against his lips, letting him know she wanted more. She craved more. His thick fingers traveled up her waist, lifting her shirt above her breasts. She felt his hands unclasp her bra, tossing it across the room. He left a trail of kisses down her neck to her collarbone. She let her gaze wander down the space between them to the thick bulge in his pants. Closing her eyes, she arched into him as he teasingly nibbled her right nipple.

"Alek," she whispered, and he smiled against her skin.

"Well, I only had enough change for two of us to get caffeine." Bridget let out a high-pitched yip, and Eva's eyes flew open. "Oh! Sorry, sorry. I, uh, I think I forgot something in the hall." Eva heard Bridget leave, then immediately reopen the door. "After you put your clothes on, I'm totally high-fiving you, Eva. That's my girl!" The door closed for good this time, and Eva covered her blazing cheeks with her hands.

"How long do you think she will be gone?" Alek asked.

"Not long enough. At least, I'd hope not." Eva pulled her shirt down and wiggled out from under him. "But this is probably for the best. So much is going on with the police, and now the Nosoi. We shouldn't make it more complicated by adding sex to the mix."

"Are you certain that is your decision?" He leaned in and pressed his lips to hers. Desire swelled within her as his tongue explored hers.

Bridget cleared her throat. "This may be a shock, but I find sex to be an amazing stress reliever. Not better than a Xanax and a little booze, but really, what is?"

Eva pulled away from Alek and cast a sideways glance at Bridget.

"Yeah, I've been standing here awhile." She grinned.

"And you are so not helping," Eva sighed.

"Yes, yes I am. I have the books." Bridget struggled to lift the Whole Foods tote she'd crammed the remaining three books into.

Thankful for the distraction, Eva hurried to Bridget and snatched the heavy bag from her grip. "Alek, we need to go through these and find anything that might help us."

"But first," Bridget said, her Coke bottle hissing as she twisted the cap, "you need to find your bra. I mean, seriously, those things are all free and jiggling around like two fat puppies."

Alek chuckled lowly at Bridget's comment. Eva ignored them both, and plucked her bra from where it landed on the back of one of the dining room chairs. "When I come back, we're figuring out how to defeat those bastards, and I don't care if it takes all night." Hopeful for the future, and warmed by the saltiness of Alek's skin still lingering on her lips, she marched into Bridget's bedroom with a smile.

TWENTY-FOUR

James chewed on the end of his pen and stared blankly at the open file on his desk. "You've got to be fucking kidding me," he moaned, and dropped his head into his palms. "Immortal warriors, Tartarus, Oracles, infections escaped from the Underworld. There's no way any of this is true. I'm dreaming. I have to be. The longest, shittiest dream I've ever had, but that's okay as long as none of this is real." A paperclip bounced off his knuckles, and he glanced up to see Schilling glaring at him from across his desk.

"Is mumbling to yourself helping our case?"

James sighed. "Doesn't seem to be."

"Well, I've been shouting at your rookie ass for at least five minutes. I talked to the captain a bit ago and we've got one hell of a day ahead of us, starting off with a visit to Pierce's office. Seems like all the shit that went down last night is connected to our case."

"The Kostas case?" James asked, trying to divert focus from what had happened at the hospital. "No, I'm sure it's not. I mean, how could that be possible?"

"Beats me, seeing as we've put that investigation on hold until we're able to find more evidence, or one of the suspects."

"Yeah, I know. I was just…."

"Dreaming? Maybe about whatever the hell happened out in the park that you're still refusing to let slip?" Schilling pried.

James averted eye contact with his partner and busied himself with the papers on his desk.

"I'm going to ignore the fact that you're still holding out. Wouldn't want you to break up with me again," Schilling snickered. "Let's head over and see Pierce. She's got our bodies, and we're not getting anything done sitting on our asses."

James abandoned his plan to keep the hospital talk off-limits and asked, "But word is what happened last night at St. John's was all because of some nasty bug. Hospitals *are* breeding grounds for all sorts of bad stuff. We're homicide. What does that have to do with us?"

"Captain put it to me like this. We owe him for fucking up the Kostas case, and this mess didn't start at the hospital. It started with Tyson George, and it's our job to figure out why, which brings us back to possible homicide. Plus, he doesn't want our department getting squeezed out of all of this by some hospital bureaucrats or the CDC or whoever's going to pop up next and lay claim."

"Wait, the CDC could be involved in this? The actual Center for Disease Control?" A pit formed in James's stomach.

"Who do you expect to come to town when some nasty

bug, as you called it, practically decimates an entire hospital? You were there. You should know how serious this is."

"I didn't go inside or anything. Stayed strictly on the perimeter," he lied. "Hey, what about contacting Monica and Tyson's friends and families? We skipping that today?" James held his breath, and hoped Schilling took the bait and changed the subject.

"You know me better than that, rookie. I don't skip. Winslow's got 'em covered," Schilling grunted as he hefted himself out of his chair.

"You're letting Winslow actually talk to people who knew Monica Carroll? Have you sat in on him questioning anyone before? He asks questions like he's on a terrible first date." James rolled his chair under his desk and joined his partner.

"Relax. I give him a hard time, and he usually deserves it, but he's got a good head on his shoulders."

The drive to the ME's office seemed longer than usual. Schilling babbled incessantly about his empty stomach, while James said a silent prayer that he and his new gang of somewhat super heroes would destroy this plague before the CDC or anyone else could get involved. He let out a deep sigh as his partner finally maneuvered the car into the wide parking lot.

"At least it's not hot as fucking hell," Schilling griped as they shuffled to the entrance.

James hesitated a moment before opening the door to the ME's office. Nothing positive was ever waiting for him within the antiseptic walls. He readied himself and slipped inside.

"*Hola,*" Veronica purred.

"You're back behind the desk." Schilling scooted around James and quickly waddled over to the attractive brunette's station. "I'd hoped you'd get to stay out in the field longer."

"So did I, but Kirby is back, and I have been banished." A pout pushed out her plump bottom lip. "But it is good to see you, Tom. And James, you're looking *muy guapo* today."

"Thanks, Vee. You're looking handsome too." James grinned at his ability to translate elementary Spanish. "Or, wait, no. You look—your top, it's very…." The fabric of her teal blouse stretched across her chest. Its small pearl buttons seemed to cling to the threads for dear life. "Big. Blue! Blue is what I meant to say. Your top is very blue."

Schilling leaned into James and mumbled, "Now who sounds like they're on an awkward first date?"

"Anyway, I'm going to go back now. It'd be great if you could let Pierce know we're here," James said, making a hasty getaway.

Schilling burst through the swinging double doors after him, laughing heartily.

"Every time I come out here you two are giggling like it's social hour." Pierce crossed her arms over her chest and propped the door open with her foot. "Who knew investigating murder was so much fun? Clearly, I chose the wrong profession." She waited for them to enter before continuing. "The majority of bodies are being held at St. John's, and the few we have here are under tight quarantine. We're still collecting samples and running tests on the victims, including the original two from Terwilleger Heights. Nothing's come back yet, but I didn't expect it to so soon. However, I can tell you that Monica Carroll's cause of death, the blunt force trauma to her skull, was sustained in a fight with her husband, Tyson George."

"So the techs were able to recover a murder weapon?" Schilling asked.

"Not exactly." She paused to shake the loose strands of hair away from her eyes. "He used his fists."

"You're kidding," Schilling grumbled.

"Afraid not. I performed both autopsies myself, and reviewed my findings multiple times. I followed the evidence, and the evidence points to Tyson George."

"But you've seen her face, Pierce. How could he possibly have done that?" Schilling asked, astounded.

James thought back to the hospital, to the doctor, her rabid attempts to get at PJ even after he'd fired two bullets into her body.

"My original guess was some kind of drug. PCP, bath salts, or another drug like that. His tox screen hasn't come back yet, so I don't know for sure that he wasn't on anything. However, with what happened at the hospital, it's pretty safe to say drugs are off the table."

"So, if he did this to her," Schilling contemplated aloud as he flipped through the photos of Monica's mangled face, "there's no way she could have retaliated, attacked him, and caused all of that." He pulled out Tyson's picture and tossed it on top of the pile.

"No fist fight, no matter how intense, would produce those effects," Pierce said.

"Since you're pretty positive this isn't drug related, what do you think it is?" James asked, pulling as much information from her as he could without arousing suspicion.

Pierce shrugged. "Some of the aspects hint at rabies, but others I've never seen before. At least, not all together like this. Also, I'm having a hard time with cause of death. Tyson's lungs were almost completely liquefied, and his trachea was practically torn to bits. Not to mention the obvious trauma to his face."

"That's putting it mildly," Schilling mumbled.

"And he's not the only one it happened to. The only way I can explain it is that something got into his lungs and each of the other victims', and then forced its way out again."

The scarlet cloud cloaked James's thoughts, and the memory of their pulsing buzz tickled his eardrums.

"I'm not following," Schilling said.

"It's like when you shake up a bottle of pop then unscrew the cap. It shoots out everywhere," James tried to explain.

"Something shook this guy until he exploded? I thought he died from going splat on the patio." Schilling's brow furrowed.

"No. Well, maybe. The two happened within such a close timeframe, it's a toss up as to which actually killed him. But whatever he inhaled rushed out of his lungs with a massive amount of force. It not only tore apart the soft tissue, it also dislocated his mandible and lacerated the flesh around his mouth. Which is exactly what happened to these other victims." She plopped down a file onto the empty exam table and spread out its contents.

James grimaced as Pierce lined up pictures of the hospital victims.

"Ugh," Schilling grunted. "Same facial…."

"Explosion," James whispered.

He nodded his head in agreement. "Yep, sounds about right."

"At first glance, yes, which is how I knew the cases were

connected. But there are a few slight differences. Their lung tissue and trachea aren't nearly as destroyed, and the damage to each of their oral cavities is much less severe. But the jury's still out on cause of death."

"But the jaws, they're all still…." James lost his words as his eyes locked on one of the photographs.

"Dislocated? Yes."

"Well, this is a fucking mess if I've ever seen one." Schilling scratched his rotund midsection. "Okay, we have to start at the beginning, with Tyson George. We're not taking the drug idea off the table. At least not until we hear about the test results. We'll start looking into anyone dealing higher-level drugs. There's also this new synthetic one making the rounds that I've been reading about. Flakka, or something. I didn't think it had gotten here yet, but looking at this makes me think I might be wrong about that. Graham, send a note to Winslow. Tell him to pull the list of top dealers operating in the area, as well as George and Carroll's financial records. We need to see if either of them made any big deposits or withdrawals, or has any outstanding debts."

Schilling's voice faded into the distance as James stared at the unnatural facial shapes in each picture.

"Dammit Graham, pull your head out of your ass," Schilling bellowed.

James blinked a few times and looked around the room as if he'd just woken up. "Yeah, I'm on it." He pulled out his phone. "E-mailing Winslow now."

Schilling cleared his throat and turned his attention back toward Catherine. "Pierce, thanks for calling us down and sharing this with us. The chain of command might be changing here soon, and we'd appreciate it if you'd keep us in the loop."

"Don't mention it. If everything wasn't being locked up so tight, I would've called you while I was at the scene. But I was instructed not to say a word. I'm sticking my neck out telling you now."

"We both owe you for this, and for whatever you decide to share with us later on," James said.

"A lot of the big hush-hush is because of legal and medical shit I want nothing to do with, but it sure doesn't help that this case is coming right on the heels of the Kostas debacle. A lot of unanswered questions with that one, let me tell you."

"Winslow's on it," James interrupted before Schilling had a chance to question him again about Mohawk Park. "We'd best get back. I'm sure there are a lot of names we need to go through. Oh, Pierce, one more thing. You think the CDC will be brought in on this?"

"I'd be surprised if they weren't already called. It's just a matter of time when dealing with a potential outbreak like this one."

James's stomach flip-flopped. "Good to know."

"We'll get out of your hair then Pierce. Give Vee a kiss for me, and two from puppy dog eyes over there," Schilling chuckled, and pointed to James.

"Don't tempt me, Schilling." Pierce's blue eyes glinted as a smirk curled her lips.

"We are not starting this again. I'm outta here. I'll be at the car." James waved goodbye over his shoulder and pushed open the door. Luckily, Veronica's back was turned and she was too preoccupied cackling on the phone to notice James tiptoeing out the front door.

"That was a nightmare. And the CDC. Jesus Christ." He sighed and leaned against the trunk of Schilling's Buick. Fall was in the air, cooling the breeze as it swirled around him.

"I see you dodged Vee on your way out," Schilling twanged. "She told me to let you know that she has an extra ticket to the movies this weekend. Guess her sister's bailing on her or something. She's hard to understand sometimes, but, woowee, is that accent something else." Schilling started the car and maneuvered out onto the busy street.

"Hey, Schilling, the station's back that way." James pointed as Schilling pulled through the next intersection.

"We're not going to the station just yet. We're going to my house for an early lunch. And just in time, too. I could reach up a hog's ass and pull out a ham sandwich I'm so hungry. I wrote you a text yesterday about coming over, remember?"

James thought back. "No, but I left my phone in my car, and I just got it back when I came in this morning."

"Well, I sent it. You didn't say anything back, but it was sent out either way."

"If someone doesn't respond to your text, you can't take that as a yes," James said.

"Oh, so sorry. That's my fault. I didn't realize your schedule was so demanding. Tell me, what exactly were your plans this afternoon? Because I thought eating some good home cooking would be loads better than staring at dead bodies or sifting through files all day, but that may just be my old age talking."

James remained silent.

"You're quiet again, and I'm taking it as you being compliant," Schilling said.

"Yeah, well, I do owe you. I just didn't think you'd be

collecting so soon."

"How about we keep that fact between the two of us. My wife won't take too kindly to being a bartering chip." Schilling's phone blared, and he swerved into oncoming traffic as he shifted his body to dig it out of his back pocket. "This is Schilling," he grumbled, and held the phone over the center console.

"Detective, it's Winslow." The young man's chipper tone grated against James's increasingly frayed nerves. "I've got a witness for you. He's in pretty bad shape up at St. Francis Hospital, and has a few screws loose from what I've heard, but he's ready to talk."

James's forehead pinched. "A witness?"

"Yeah, I guess someone made it out of St. John's last night and headed over to a bar on Brookside," Winslow answered. "Apparently this guy was the only one left standing after he got through."

"And why are we just now hearing about this?" Schilling questioned.

"That was the very first question I asked when I got the call, Detective." Winslow's grin beamed through his words. "The nurse said our guy got lost in the shuffle. I guess he was freaking out, spouting all sorts of crazy talk, so they put him on a psychiatric hold. They brought him down from the psych floor a little bit ago. It wasn't until then that he calmed down and they figured out he wasn't some ordinary ER admit. Captain Alvarez wants you two to go up there and talk to him ASAP."

"So much for lunch." James bit the inside of his cheek to keep from smiling with relief.

• • •

James impatiently bounced his foot against the speckled tile floor of St. Francis Hospital. "You'd think having a badge would speed this process along."

"The whole world is full of hurry up and wait," Schilling groaned. "But if I would've known it was going to take so goddamn long, we could've at least pulled through a Wendy's."

"So sorry to keep you waiting," a young nurse greeted them. Her strawberry blonde bangs skimmed the tops of her eyebrows as she spoke. "Mr. Dennison had a little bit of a moment, and needed to calm down before he was able to talk with you. The doctor did green-light a sedative, but I only administered a small dose, so he's still coherent enough to answer your questions. If you'll follow me, I'll take you right to him." She adjusted her snug top and brushed her ponytail off of her shoulder. "Oh, and I also have to apologize for the small mix-up and not contacting you sooner. We've been swamped. Although, talking to him earlier just wouldn't have been possible."

"You said he needed to calm down. This isn't related to his overnight stay on the crazy floor of the hospital?" Schilling asked.

"We prefer to call it the psychiatric floor, Detective," she said, casting a sideways glance at the grumbly man. "But yes. Mr. Dennison has had a little bit of a problem distinguishing frightening science fiction from reality. He's been quite the mess."

"Great," Schilling mumbled.

"This is Mr. Dennison's room." She paused in front of

the closed wooden door and peered in through the small window. "A few minor quarantine precautions are in place, which you'll notice upon entry. If there is any problem at all, you can press the red button on the wall or just leave the room. I'll wait out here for you in case there's any trouble."

"Hate to say it, but you're not making me feel at ease about going in there," James said.

"Well." She cleared her throat and plastered on an eerie, fake grin. "I'm sure everything will be just fine. And when you're finished with your talk, I can take you to visit with the doctor. She has more information on Mr. Dennison's mental state and the physical injuries he had when he arrived."

Schilling stepped back and motioned to the door. "On that note, you take the mental patient. I'll go find out what the doc knows. Mainly, how this whole fuckup happened in the first place."

"Yeah, no problem." Unsure of what to expect, James opened the door and stepped into the sterile hospital room. Plastic hung around the hospital bed, and hissing tubes stuck out of the clear, crinkled plastic-like quills on a porcupine. Anthony Dennison lay quietly on top of the wrinkled white sheets. Ashy grey tinted his skin like a fresh coat of slick lacquer. Sweat soaked through his hospital gown, darkening the yellowish fabric so much that it matched his pallor.

"Anthony Dennison?" The name came out as a whisper, and James cleared his throat and tried again. "Anthony Dennison?"

The man's eyes fluttered open, and he nodded sleepily. "That's me."

The room was unnervingly silent as James stepped closer to the bed. "Mr. Dennison, I'd like to ask you a few questions about what happened last night at The Brook."

"Sabrina," he murmured, a faint smile flitting across his lips.

"Sabrina?" James pulled out his phone and scrolled through the list of victims from the bar. "Yes, Sabrina Masten was there. Can you tell me what happened last night?"

Fluorescent lights glinted off his glassy expression as he stared up at James. "I know the truth. I know what happened. You won't believe me."

"Try me. I think you'll be surprised."

"But this isn't *normal*. They think…." He lifted his head off the pillow and peered around James. His expression changed and, comfortable with what he saw, he settled back against the bedding. "They think I'm crazy."

James grabbed the chair from the corner of the room and slid it next to the bed. "If I told people what I've seen in the past few days, they'd think I'm crazy too. There's no judgment here. It's safe to talk."

"Something was inside of her," Anthony whispered. "Inside Sabrina."

"What do you mean?" James leaned in closer.

"She was different. Violent. Crazy. *They* made her that way."

"They? They who?"

Anthony pursed his lips and fixed his gaze on the door's small window.

"Anthony," James said, drawing the man's attention back to him. "Who? Who made Sabrina different?"

Tears leaked from the corners of his marble eyes. "The swarm." He pressed his thighs against his chest until his body resembled a muscular ball. "The scarlet rain."

"Scarlet rain." Images of Tyson's death and the pulsing cloud at St. John's stirred within James.

"They made her do the things she did. They made her cut me." He fingered the bandage sticking out of the top of his gown. "But I pushed her. I shouldn't have, but I did." He tucked his chin against his knees and moaned softly.

"It's okay, Anthony. Tell me more about the swarm. Did you see it?"

He shook his head. "I don't want to talk anymore. I'm not crazy. I'm not. I promise."

"I know. I don't think you're crazy, Anthony. I believe you."

"Don't lie to me."

"I'm not."

Anthony closed his eyes and rocked gently against his pillow.

"Okay." James gripped the seat of his chair and scooted closer to the bed. He leaned in, his face only inches away from the plastic, and said, "I've seen them too."

Anthony cracked his eyelids and peered up at James. His tear-streaked face and pale complexion softened his otherwise burly form. "I'm not crazy. They said I am, but I'm not. You've seen them too."

"Yes, I have. Now, tell me what you saw."

Anthony recounted his story from the bar, gradually growing more comfortable, speaking hesitantly, then more openly. His breath caught as he described the carnage.

James's phone chimed, making both men flinch. He opened the text from Pierce and read it quickly. *Tox screens coming in. All results neg so far. Sending blood work from the office to CDC first thing Monday.*

"Okay, Anthony. Listen to me. I have to go."

"You're not going to tell them what I told you, are you?" Childlike fear flashed across Anthony's face.

"I won't tell anyone, and I suggest you do the same. Keep your mouth shut and forget this ever happened, unless you want to spend the rest of your life locked in the psych ward."

"But what about Sabrina? Did I kill her?"

James stood and tucked his phone into his pocket. "No, Anthony. She was dead before you left the bathroom."

"Detective." He crept closer to the plastic and whispered, "The queen is coming." Anthony rocked onto his back and nodded listlessly. "The queen is coming."

TWENTY-FIVE

Eva rested her forehead on the pages of the open book. The earthy scent of old leather tickled her nose, and she stifled a sneeze before groaning, "I can't believe we watched the sunrise, and it's dark again already. I'm pretty sure we've been awake for more than twenty-four hours. What time is it anyway?" She glanced up at Alek, who was studiously flipping through the pages of one of the massive hardbacks. His eyes had dulled and his skin was matte and colorless.

"Are you okay?" she asked.

"I am well." He smiled weakly and turned his attention to the living room. "Perhaps Bridget knows the time."

The couch hid Bridget's body, so Eva stared at the curly blonde ponytail draped over the decorative pillows. "Bridge, what time is it?" The ponytail didn't move. "Bridget!"

She popped up from the couch like a meerkat. "You rang."

"What time is it? I feel like we've been at this forever," Eva said.

Bridget rubbed her eyes and dug her phone out from under her. "It's way past happy hour. This has my sleep schedule all messed up. Any luck?"

Alek shook his head. "So far we have found nothing useful."

"But there's still one to go through." Eva reached across the table and pulled the last of the hardbacks toward her. The flaking silver paint of the five-pointed star seemed to twinkle up at her from the cracked leather cover. "Fourth one's the charm, I guess." She plopped down in her chair and let her gaze linger on Alek. She'd seen him look like this before, when they were in Mohawk Park. Worry knotted her stomach. "Alek, you don't look so great. Are you really feeling okay?"

He took a deep breath, his shoulders slumping. "I want to be here and find something that might help us, but I think it's time I return to Tartarus. I have not been in this realm long, but I have put my body through much."

"You don't have to explain. Go get your strength back, any by the time you return I'll have figured out something that will help us."

"Are you sure you do not need me to stay?" He used the table to steady himself as he shakily walked to Eva.

"I need you to do a lot of things, but you're no use to me without any energy." She bit the corner of her lip.

"I'll make sure to address each of those needs once I am back." He smirked.

Eva pushed herself up on her tiptoes and wrapped her arms around his neck. "You better."

He kissed her softly before backing up a few paces. "I'll return to you soon." He gripped his talisman. The air around him twinkled, and a sharp gust blew through the condo.

"Bye, Alek." Eva smiled at the fading warrior and slid down into her chair. She huffed and turned to the first brittle page of the thick book, reading the title aloud. "Spells and potions. Whoa, I actually get to do spells? There has to be something in here we can use." She scoured page after page of ancient writings, getting lost in the lyrical prose of the Oracles who'd come before her.

Bridget's phone blared, pulling Eva from the magic scrawled on each page.

"*Hola,*" Bridget said, with a surprising amount of enthusiasm for someone who'd been snoring only minutes before. "James, slow down. I can't understand you." Eva's stomach dropped as concern wrinkled Bridget's brow. "Wait, I'm going to put you on speaker so Eva can hear." She pushed herself up off the couch and shuffled to the table. "Okay, repeat what you just said."

"The medical examiner is sending out some samples to the CDC first thing Monday. They're the big guns in charge of nasty diseases, which is what we have on our hands," he explained.

Eva's thoughts swirled while she envisioned the outcome of involving the CDC. "Even if they could identify and create a vaccine for whatever illness the Nosoi are creating, it wouldn't do any good. They'd just come up with some other horrible disease to use to wipe us out."

"And you know they'd love it too," Bridget added. "That's what the Furies were talking about, how humans will use science and fight to stay alive. Those little Nosoi bastards would just fly around laughing at us. Well, if laughing is something they do."

Eva lowered her face toward the phone, as if getting closer would increase the urgency in her voice. "James, can't you talk to someone and buy us more time?"

"I've already spent hours talking to my partner, the medical examiner, even my captain. Right now I'm fighting just to stay in the know on this. I'm sorry, but there's nothing I can do."

"But there might be something *I* can do." Eva frantically flipped through the book and stopped when she came across the page with a large oval encircling a short spell and a symbol of what looked like a bow and arrow. "James, I know you said you're out of options, but maybe you're not thinking about this creatively enough. Work your own kind of magic and figure something out."

"Yeah, we have faith in you." Bridget beamed. "We also need a plan B in case we totally fail."

Eva pursed her lips. "Let us know if you figure something out or hear anything else. Right now there's something I have to go do. We'll call you back." She reached across Bridget, and ended the call before sliding the book closer to her friend. "I'm doing this." She pointed to the bubble in the middle of the page.

Bridget squinted. "I can't read it, remember?"

"Oh, right. It's a protection spell. It forms some kind of impenetrable bubble around whatever needs to be kept safe."

"So what are you going to try and put a bubble around?" Bridget asked.

"Tulsa."

Bridget snorted. "Wait, you're serious?"

"Absolutely. There doesn't seem to be anything James can do to get to those samples, and we have no idea what info the CDC may already have. Plus, we need the Nosoi to stay in the city. We'll never be able to stop them if they're free to fly around wherever they want."

"All good points, but have you ever done a spell before?"

"Well, no. But I also wasn't the Oracle before."

"Another good point. Okay, let's gather up everything you'll need and you can go all Glinda the Good Witch on this stuff as soon as Alek gets back."

"I can't wait that long. I've been so focused on what's going on with us right here that I haven't stopped to think about the rest of the world. Maiden said they're drawn to me, which puts us at an advantage, and right now the Nosoi don't have a lot of power, but we don't know when that will change. I can't give them the opportunity to get ahead of us more than they have already. It's for the greater good, and I know Alek will understand." Eva read over the short list of supplies and bookmarked the page she needed.

"Fine," Bridget groaned. "This goes against my better judgment, but I can tell you're not going to change your mind. I'll get my keys."

"I appreciate it, but you're not coming. Someone has to be here to tell Alek what's going on."

"I don't let just anyone drive my car," Bridget said, tossing Eva her keys. "You're lucky you're like my sister, and I totally trust you."

Eva slipped on the jacket she'd worn to burglarize her house, and tightened the hood around her face. "I'll be sure to obey the speed limit so I don't get in a wreck."

"Or pulled over and thrown in jail."

"Don't remind me." She rested the heavy book on her hip and dropped the keys into her pocket. "And don't worry.

It's all written out for me. The book says I have to find a place of circle and stone, and of iron and energy, that echoes with the wisdom of ages. Whatever that means."

"I don't know about the iron or energy or any of that, but I do know of someplace that echoes—the Center of the Universe. In high school, Vodka Bridget used to go there and tell herself how awesome she was. You are awesome! Awesome…. Awesome…." She giggled.

"See, it's working out perfectly. Nothing's going to go wrong."

TWENTY-SIX

"Alek." Crone's soothing, earthy scents reached him as the great hall settled around him.

"Crone." He let out a relieved sigh. "I am glad it is you."

The creases around her eyes deepened with her smile. "And I am glad to see you well, my son." She nodded and returned her attention to the scrolls littering the wide stone table in front of her.

Alek relaxed into the intoxicating sensation creeping up his feet and surging through his body. The dull pulsing from his bruised muscles diminished. Refilled with the energy of his home, he pulled out a chair and sat across from his eldest mother. "Do you wish to know what is taking place in the Mortal Realm?"

Her eyes didn't lift from her reading. "Only if you wish to inform me."

There was comfort in her lack of prodding. "And if I do not?"

"Then we shall sit in silence. It can be very healing, letting your senses relax from the onslaught of noise present in the Mortal Realm. And you are grown. If you have something to tell me, I trust you will make yourself heard."

"I wish this was something you could teach to your sisters," he mumbled.

Crone smiled. "They would bicker over the color of rocks if they thought the fight could be won."

"Alek, I thought I sensed your presence." Mother wrapped a shawl around her slender frame as she hurried into the hall. "Have you come to inform us of your strategy to defeat the Nosoi?"

"No, Mother. I'm here to regain my strength so I am *able* to defeat them." His jaw muscles tightened as he bit back his annoyance.

"But what of your plan? Which tactics will you employ to assure their demise?" she asked.

"I am uncertain. The Oracle is searching the Tomes as we speak. She will find a way to end them, or at least slow them down."

"Slow them down? Maiden, Crone, and I are taking turns watching the Nosoi still jailed within this realm. They are awake for the first time in decades. It will not be long until the swarm in the Mortal Realm has absorbed enough energy to call upon those left behind. They *will* escape. It is time to take decisive action, not simply slow them down. I am sure Crone will agree with my sentiment."

Again Crone spoke without moving her gaze. "Alek is aware of what must be done. Other than that, I have no thoughts on the matter."

"Good, because I need no more opinions. This does not fall on you." He turned to face Mother. "Any of you. It's my task, and I will succeed without being interrogated each time I return."

"Alek," Mother began.

"No more, Mother." He pounded the table with his fist. "I only want to know you'll respect what I have said."

"As warrior of this realm, I will always respect your word." Her brow wrinkled and she stared at him more intently. "What I have to say is not about the Mortal Realm."

Crone set down her pages and stared at Alek. "It is your talisman."

He glanced down at the cracked crystal resting against his chest. It glowed brilliant amber in the dim cavern.

"What kind of power is this?" Mother asked. "It is one I have never seen before."

"It's Eva. She is the only one who can affect it in this way. I must go to her." He pinched the crystal between his thumb and forefinger and, without the help of the Furies, disappeared from Tartarus.

• • •

"Think creatively." James dropped his forehead into his hands and stared down at his desk. Almost everyone had gone home for the night, which was perfect for the young detective. Now he didn't have to worry about bored, nosy cops—or worse, his partner. "There has to be a way I can get into Pierce's office and to those samples." He studied the stacks of files and various papers neatly placed in labeled trays, and let his gaze wander the pile of magazines he'd swiped from the bathroom. An old issue of Wired Magazine poked out from the stack, and James silently read the exposed text. *"How George Lucas changed movies forever."*

"Definitely not something I would know. I haven't been to a movie in ages." Schilling's twang rolled around in his memory as the beginnings of a plan emerged. "That's it. That's how I can get in." He dug into his pocket, pulled out his phone, and texted Pierce.

What's Veronica's number? he typed, and sent the question before glancing up at the clock and adding, *Sorry it's so late.*

Pierce responded almost immediately with Veronica's number and the words *"GOOD LUCK"* in all caps.

James composed a short message inquiring about the movie Schilling said Veronica invited him to, and clicked send before he had the chance to talk himself out of his ingenious, although not-very-well-thought-out plan. Minutes ticked by agonizingly slowly while he stared at the screen, waiting for her to reply. "She's probably asleep or out. This was a stupid idea." He sighed and dropped his phone onto his desk. It vibrated loudly against the wooden surface. He scooped it up and rushed to read her response.

Glad you want to come! Movie is on Sunday. I'm downtown with friends. Want to come out for a drink?

"Maybe this isn't so stupid after all." He smiled to himself and typed a reply asking where to meet up.

"Now how's that for thinking creatively?" With a somewhat-thought-out plan for how to gain access to Pierce's office, James gathered his things and headed for his car.

Twenty-Seven

James turned the stereo up and drove the short distance to where Veronica and her friends were waiting at Vintage 1740. James had only been in the cozy wine bar twice before. Both times on awkward first dates that led nowhere. Hopefully, on this trip, he'd be able to suss out a way into Veronica's workplace without creating too much suspicion. He maneuvered his car into the narrow strip of the last parking space in front of the bar, and punched out a quick update to Bridget.

Coming in from the brightly lit street, his eyes adjusted to the romantic glow emanating from the wine bottle fixtures.

"Detective James. Please, sit." Veronica motioned to the empty seat next to her at the bar.

His leg grazed hers as he slid onto the stool, arousing the bundle of nerves he'd managed to keep under control until now. "Please, call me James. Just James."

The golden light pouring from the backlit bar display deepened her skin tone to an even richer shade of caramel.

"Okay, just James. I am glad you came. The notice I gave was so short."

"I'm glad I came too." He looked around, expecting to see at least one person he needed to introduce himself to. "Where are your friends?"

"I have a confession." She averted her eyes and traced the rim of her nearly empty glass. "I knew they were leaving, but I wanted you to meet me, so I told a small lie and said they were still here. I didn't want you to be scared of being alone with me."

"Me, scared of you? That doesn't sound like me. Not at all. Nope. Not. At. All." He tugged at his rigid shirt collar and smiled awkwardly. "I think intimidated is the word you're looking for."

Wrinkles formed on the bridge of her nose as she laughed. "Are you going to get a drink? We are at this beautiful bar filled with wines, and you are without a glass."

"Wish I could, but I can't. Have to stay sharp. A detective's job is never done," he chuckled stiffly.

"And I'm sure you are an amazing detective," she purred, and locked her gaze with his.

"Yes. I, uh."

She delicately placed her palm on his thigh and slid it up and down his leg.

"I fight lots of crime." He let his eyes sweep over her killer figure one final time before clearing his throat and bringing himself back on task. "Speaking of jobs, you guys must have some tight security over at the office, what with all the personal effects you handle."

She brought her hand back to her glass and took a sip. "Not really. I just swipe my card and enter the one one one

one on the number buttons, and it stops the beeping."

"Oh, you need a keycard to enter," he said, more to himself than Veronica. "That's more than I expected."

"But I don't want to talk about work. I come here to forget work and—" Her shoulders bounced, and she politely covered her mouth with her fingertips. "*Lo siento.* My stomach has not been well, and now it is very angry." Beads of sweat sprouted on her smooth forehead, and she used her free hand to fan her face.

"Are you okay?" James asked.

Veronica heaved forward, clenching her stomach and shaking her head. "No, I—" Again she lurched forward. This time her hand shot up and clamped over her lips. Eyes wide, she hopped off the barstool and darted off in the direction of the restroom.

James ordered a glass of ginger ale and went over his plan as he waited for Veronica to return. *Meet with Veronica. Check. Figure out security at Pierce's office. Check. Gain access to office. I'm marking that as a half check. There's still time. It could happen.* He glanced at his phone. No word back from Bridget. He hoped her plans were going more smoothly than his own.

"I am very sorry for being sick." Veronica collapsed onto the barstool and dabbed her face with a stray cocktail napkin. The richness of her brown skin was overtaken by a sickly green, and sweat shimmered on her face and chest. "It was the oysters. *Mi madre* always said, 'do not eat food that carries around its house.' I should have listened."

James stifled a cringe. "Food poisoning. That's the worst. If you're sick, you can go. Don't stay here because of me."

"I would love to leave, but I must ask a favor. I have no car here. You will drive me home?"

"Yeah, sure. Definitely." He set some cash on the bar for the full soda, and led Veronica out the front door. "My car's right here."

"*Gracias.*" She shakily fell into the passenger seat.

James closed the door and rounded the car, patting down his pockets for the pack of gum he usually kept in his jacket. "Here." He offered her the foil-wrapped stick, and smiled apologetically.

"Ah, *sí*. You've come prepared." A weak grin momentarily brightened her eyes.

The drive to Veronica's house was mostly silent, except for the succinct directions she offered.

"I didn't realize you lived so close to where you work." James let his car idle in the driveway.

"Easy commute." She dug the garage door opener out of her purse, and pressed the button. "Thank you, James. You are a very nice man. Just like Tom said."

"Schilling said that? Huh. Well, it's really no problem. I hope you start to feel better."

Her stomach growled so loud it made James grimace. "Oh, no," she muttered.

"You sure you're going to be okay?"

Without answering, she kicked off her stilettos and darted into the open garage.

"Okay, I'll get those for you." He collected her spiky heels from the footwell, and trotted into the garage after her. Stiffly, he stepped into the kitchen and closed the door behind him. A hall light illuminated the way to the bathroom, and he set the shoes down outside the door. "Just going to leave these outside here." The sound of Veronica retching made his stomach turn. "So, I'm going to go and leave you to it." He waited for a response, but only heard more heaving. "Okay, I'll text you." He retraced his steps back to the kitchen, but paused before leaving. Veronica's ID card swung listlessly from the key hook next to the door. He unhooked the lanyard and turned the card over. A magnetic strip ran across the empty white expanse of the back of the card, and James couldn't help but grin. *It's still a go.*

"Hey, Veronica!" he hollered again. "Changed my mind. I'm going to run out for a sec and get you some stuff from the store to help you feel better. I'll be back soon." He quietly slipped the card into his jacket pocket and bounded out to his car. A baleful wave of anxiety rushed through him as every mile brought him closer to Pierce's office.

"This is not illegal, James. You're not doing anything wrong. Well, technically yes, it *is* illegal, and I've already broken a number of laws. Shit." He turned off his lights and coasted into the parking lot. "Okay, don't think of this act of burglary as a blatant disregard for your career and everything you swore to uphold. You're here to save the planet and all the realms. Kind of like an Avenger. And people, for the most part, like the Avengers. You're doing the right thing here, James. Good pep talk." He turned off his car and dug a ball cap out from under the gym bag in the backseat. There was no way he was about to risk getting spotted. He liked his job and his freedom too much and, with friends like Bridget and Eva, he needed to stay on the right side of the law.

Protected by his hat, and feeling a bit like a vigilante, James slinked over to the front doors of the medical examiner's office. He pulled out his phone, turned on the flashlight, and hunted for a place to slide Veronica's ID card. A metal box was affixed to the building, and James swiped the stolen card and pressed the "one" button four times like Veronica had said. The light flashed from red to green. James yanked open the door and entered the same lobby he'd been in earlier that day. The alarm beeped rapidly, and James searched feverishly for a way to disarm it. He skidded to a stop in front of the keypad and, with a slightly trembling hand, passed Veronica's card through the reader and punched in her four-digit code. The alarm stopped abruptly, and James took a deep, relieved breath before pointing his flashlight in the direction of the autopsy rooms. He'd only been inside a handful of them, but remembered seeing a steel refrigerator in the area that held a bunch of expensive-looking lab equipment. He pushed through the swinging double doors and stealthily tiptoed down the hallway.

Pierce's office was always a little creepy, and rightfully so, but James never thought about what it'd be like skulking around the macabre building afterhours. With the infected from St. John's Hospital still fresh in his mind, James kept his ears perked for sounds from anything unnatural possibly lingering in the dark.

He stopped outside the familiar door, ignoring the biohazard warning signs taped to the wood. He shone his flashlight in through the narrow window, stopping when the beam of light reached the tall refrigerator. "That's it." He smiled to himself and twisted the door handle. The door to the lab was locked. "Shit." He jiggled the handle a few more times to be certain before guiding the light around the doorframe. A keypad glinted, and he typed in Veronica's code. A light flashed red and went dark. He tried the door. Still locked. "What the hell?" James punched in the number again, and again the red light flashed. "She doesn't have access to the lab. Dammit." Annoyed that he'd gotten so far only to fail, James smacked his palm against the keypad. The light flashed green and James seized the opportunity to gain entry into the lab.

A rancid odor hung in the air, and made him gag when he opted to breathe out of his mouth. He shook away his disgust, and made a beeline for the refrigerator. The soles of his shoes squeaked across the slick tile, and he held his arms out to steady himself. Before taking another step, James guided the light to the floor. Sanguine sludge coated the formerly white tiles, and he followed the puddle to its origin on the far right wall.

The metal rectangles he thought of as body lockers stretched from floor to ceiling. Red ooze dripped from the doors of several of the lockers, and James resisted his instinct to retreat back to his car. Instead, he pushed forward, ignoring the wall of bleeding steel and focusing on his ultimate destination. The narrow beam of light swept the floor around his feet as he carefully maneuvered forward. James grimaced at the wet clumps dangling off his shoes with each step toward the refrigerator.

He pulled open the heavy door, and his breath caught in his throat. The same red ooze coating the floor pooled on the top shelf and steadily dribbled down, streaking the edge of each clear ledge in its descent.

"Oh, disgusting." James shivered. "But good. This is good. These samples can't possibly be sent to the CDC now, and whatever bodies were in those lockers, well, they aren't bodies anymore. At least we don't have anything to worry about on this end."

He released the steel door and it slapped against the

frame with a hissing suction. For a moment, he stood motionless to let his eyes adjust to the gloomy black of the room.

"Shit. What am I going to do about these shoes?" The detective in him, and his reemerging common sense, wouldn't let him walk out into the hall and leave a trail of bloody footprints that screamed, "Look! Somebody broke in!" He panned the flashlight around the room and slid over to the glinting paper towel dispenser. Stuffing as many as he could into his fist, James trudged back to the door. The ooze felt like sandy Jell-O and stuck to his fingers when he wiped it from his shoes. The smell seemed to get worse as more moisture stuck to his hands, and he swallowed against the bile building in his throat.

With his feet as clean as they would get, James balled up the paper towels and headed for the sink in the room he and Schilling spent the most time in. He pressed his back against the door and said a silent prayer of thanks as it swung open. He tossed the wad into the bin and rushed to the sink and twisted the tap. Steaming water splashed against the sides of the metal basin, and he plunged his hands under the warm stream.

"This better be over soon." He pumped a mound of soap into his palm and scrubbed. The last time he'd had so much blood on his hands, he'd been reluctantly helping Mel's dad dress a deer. He'd felt filthy then, but not as filthy as he did now, with images of the infected swirling in his thoughts as their blood clung to his skin. With all visible traces of his experience gone, he dried off his hands and hurried back to the keypad by the front door. He pressed the button conveniently labeled "ARM," and rushed out the double doors.

Back in the comfort of his car, he breathed deeply for what seemed like the first time since he'd made the decision to break into Pierce's domain.

Twenty-Eight

Eva made sure to abide by all traffic laws as she slowly and cautiously maneuvered Bridget's Camaro along the one-way streets of downtown Tulsa. The last thing she, or any of them, needed right now was the attention of the police.

She parked in the empty lot of the Jazz Hall of Fame, collected the book and a knife she'd swiped from Bridget's kitchen, passed the bizarre iron statue jutting its obelisk-like head into the sky, and hurried to the Center of the Universe. She stood in the middle of the worn concrete circle and opened the book at her feet. "Okay," she sighed. The word echoed back to her, and she smiled, remembering the last time she'd been to the Center of the Universe. It felt like a lifetime ago. She, her mom, and her dad had stood together in the brick circle, their laughter circling back to them in Tulsa's strange acoustic anomaly. She'd held her father's hand as they walked the same path she had walked only moments before. While they walked, he told her stories about the magic within the Center of the Universe. How it was a portal to other dimensions, and only those within the circle could hear the echo of what was being said, but everyone outside heard nothing. It was one of the few places they went as a family before her father left.

Feeling overwhelmed, she gripped the talisman and distracted herself with positive images. "Bridget, Mom, Alek." *Alek. The couch....* She smiled. "Now *that's* a positive image." Her cheeks flushed as she twirled the softly pulsing pendant hanging around her neck. The light from the crystal warmed her fingers as the gentle fall breeze turned into hefty gusts. The book's brittle pages whipped in the wind, and she slammed it closed. The sudden burst of air settled, and Alek stepped into the circle.

"Alek, what are you doing here?"

"My talisman." He released the crystal and it bounced against his chest. "It brought me to you."

"Oh." She looked down at her necklace and tucked it back into her shirt. "I guess I was holding it and thinking about you. I didn't know it would bring you here."

"But it's a good thing I have come. This does not look to be Bridget's home."

"Yeah, about that. James said the CDC are coming, and they'll be way worse than the cops. Plus, we can't let the Nosoi get out of Tulsa. We'll never be able to defeat them if they fly to some other city. And I found this protection spell, so I decided to come here and do it, thereby protecting the rest of the world with my Oracle greatness." She smiled in hopes that she wouldn't have to combat some ridiculous lecture.

"Did you choose this place because of its magic?" he asked.

"What? Oh, the echo. That's not magic. I'm pretty sure

that's science."

"There are places within each realm where the veil between realms in thinner. Your instincts have led you to such a place." He crouched down and placed his palm in the center of the circle. "Do you feel it?"

She flattened her hand on the concrete next to Alek's. The ground vibrated gently, and static tickled her fingers. "How does no one else know about this?"

"No one else here is immortal or of Oracle blood."

"But my dad knew," she whispered.

"What?"

"Nothing. Let's get this spell started so we can get back to Bridget's, and figure out how to end the Nosoi for good." She turned to the page with the protection spell, and picked up the knife. She took a deep breath and slid the blade up her forearm. Blood gushed from the wound, and she quickly coated her fingers before it closed.

"Apollo, hear me." Her words echoed back to her as she painted the symbol of the bow on the concrete. "Your Oracle is in need. Protect this city from this nightfall to the next, so that no evil may enter or exit. I beseech you, Apollo. Please, answer my plea." She finished drawing the arrow and smacked her palm against the bloody concrete. Blinding light shot out from beneath her hand, followed by a deafening boom. The earth shook, and car alarms honked in the distance.

"Look, Eva." Alek stood, his chin pointing toward the sky.

Shimmering gold light rippled above them and faded into the clouds.

"It worked. He listened." Relief washed over her as she

cradled the book in her arms and led Alek to the car. "I can't believe I just did my first spell. And nothing bad happened."

"I wouldn't say nothing." Alek motioned down the street.

Every light was extinguished, leaving Tulsa black.

Deflated, Eva dropped the book into the car and sagged against the seat. "Crap."

• • •

Eva pulled up in front of Bridget's building, and she and Alek hurried into the lobby. Since her spell had sent Tulsa into a blackout, both sets of front doors opened freely, and Eva didn't bother to check in with the front office.

"Ugh," she groaned, passing in front of the unmoving elevators. "We have to take the stairs all the way up to Bridget's place."

Alek nodded and marched to the entrance to the stairwell.

"Climbing all these stairs doesn't suck for you even just a little?" she asked.

"I welcome the challenge." A glimmer of smugness rested in Alek's grin.

"Oh, puke," Eva mumbled as she stepped into the stairwell. Fluorescent light from the emergency exit signs bathed the stairs and cast deep shadows around each corner.

"Now that you have ensured the Nosoi's containment—"

"For the next twenty-four hours," Eva interjected.

"Yes. Now that the creatures are trapped, what are we to do about defeating them?"

"I think the only thing we can do is what your mothers said worked last time: trap them inside somebody and use fire, water, or earth to kill them."

"Yes, I have come to that conclusion as well," he said, keeping up his hurried pace.

"At least we're on the same page." Eva's legs started to burn as they walked past the door leading to the fifteenth floor. "But how do we get them all into one person?"

"The missing part of the Nosoi is coming, *She* is coming, and I do not know of any follower who would be absent from their leader's return."

"She?" Eva paused and looked up at him. "Who's that?"

Alek shrugged. "I cannot be sure. But that is what the Nosoi said. This realm would be under *Her* control."

"So we have to wait until the ultimate big bad shows up? I thought the point was to stop them before it got that far."

"I do not foresee an outcome where that's possible, do you?"

Finally on the twentieth floor, Eva led the way down the hall while she thought about it for a moment. "Well, no. If there was a way, we would have done it by now."

"Then our next mission is to be present when their queen arrives in this realm."

"How in the world are we going to make sure we're around for that?" Eva punched in Bridget's lock code and stepped into the dark living room. "Bridge?" she called, but was met only with silence. With Bridget's floor plan basically memorized, Eva made it to the junk drawer in the kitchen where Bridget stored her flashlight. She clicked it on and waved it around the room.

"Ahh." Alek shielded his eyes as she flicked the bright beam across his face.

"Whoops. Sorry about that."

"Wait, bring it back," he instructed.

She passed the beam over his body, admiring how good he looked even in the unflattering lighting.

"Not on me. Over there." He pointed in the direction of the dining room table.

A white square lay in the center of the cherry wood. "She left a note." Eva picked up the paper and read Bridget's scratchy handwriting aloud. "Your mom called to see if I'd heard from you. I lied, of course. But she has this awful cough, so I'm off to pick up some cough drops and cold meds and drop them by the house. By the way, you having my car is forcing me to take a cab. I hate cabs. You owe me. Again. Xoxox, Dr. B."

"I have never heard this xoxox before. What is its meaning?" Alek asked.

"Hugs and kisses. X's are the hugs and O's are the kisses, or maybe it's the other way around. Either way, it doesn't matter right now. What's important is getting to my house. I don't like the thought of my mom being sick with no way to contact me. What if it's bronchitis or something, and she needs to go be seen by a doctor?"

"We shall make sure your mother is well. Then we must focus on the Nosoi before they overtake this realm," Alek said flatly.

"Deal." Eva rushed from the condo and whined under her breath as they passed the elevators.

Twenty-Nine

Before Alek had the chance to follow her up the porch stairs to her front door, Eva placed her hand firmly against his shoulder. The talisman warmed her chest and shone a muted gold from under her shirt when they connected. "Don't come in. I'm sorry, but you can't. As far as I know, she thinks you had something to do with my abduction, and I don't want to come up with a lie to explain why you're here. Not yet anyway."

"I understand. If you need me, I'll be here."

Dread clawed Eva's chest as she opened the door and crept into her house. The sight of her mom curled on the couch in the fetal position sucked the air from her lungs and pinned her feet to the floor. Defeat and malady had drained the color from Lori's face, and her pasty skin glistened in the candlelight. Broken capillaries colored the whites of her eyes, and her breath came in ragged whistles.

"Mom." The whisper barely snuck past Eva's lips.

"Eva, you're back," her mother wheezed, the corners

of her eyes wrinkling as she smiled weakly. "I knew you'd come home."

"I'm so sorry I didn't come sooner." She knelt next to her mom and warmed her cold, limp hand between her palms. "I just wanted to get everything figured out first. I didn't want to drag you into this craziness. I was only trying to protect you."

"Silly girl, I don't need protecting. I need my daughter." Spittle flew from her lips as she coughed. "I don't know what's wrong with me. I have no idea where I could have caught this horrible thing. I felt fine until earlier today."

Eva offered her best attempt at a smile as she brushed the damp, matted hair from Lori's eyes. "I am always telling you to get your flu shot."

"This isn't the flu, Eva. I've never felt anything like this. I have all of this anger. I think there's something seriously wrong."

"Not for long, Ms. K." Bridget squatted on the floor next to Eva and held out a steaming cup. "I made tea." She fanned the hot liquid, and gave a toothy smile before leaning into Eva. "This is bad news bears. I'm glad you got my note."

"I hear talking," Lori whispered.

Bridget and Eva exchanged confused looks.

"In my head," Lori added. "It's scaring me."

"You probably have a fever," Bridget said, sliding the mug onto the coffee table.

Eva gently felt her mom's forehead. Heat tingled against her fingertips and her stomach clenched with terrible foreboding. "Yeah, we're taking you to the hospital."

Lori lifted her head. A wet ring of tiny ruby specks stippled the fabric. Her face morphed as she pushed herself up into a sitting position. A sly smile lifted her damp, pale lips. "*There is no need. We will stay with you mortals. We have much to fix before this realm can be ours.*"

Despair froze Eva's heart. "Mom?"

"*She is here. She is fighting. She is strong. We like them strong. More power to use and to take.*" Lori seemed to deflate as she fell against the couch, her body rattling with coughs.

Bridget recoiled. "That stuff on the pillow. Those red dots. It's them, isn't it? Those things from the video and the book."

"Get Alek and call James. Then stay outside. When James shows up, tell him to do the same," Eva commanded. "I don't know what this is capable of, but I know we need all the help we can get."

Bridget scrambled toward the door.

"Something's wrong. Something's very wrong," Lori whimpered.

"I know. I know. It's fine. Everything's going to be okay." Tears bit at Eva's eyes as she stroked her mom's sweat-streaked hair. "We know someone who will help. And I'm here. I can help too."

"They're inside me, Eva. I can feel them. I can hear them talking. They want me to do horrible things." Blood trickled out of Lori's nose as she again erupted into body-shaking coughs.

"No!" Eva shouted, wiping at her eyes with the back of her sleeve. "This is not happening. I've already given up so much. They're not taking you too. Do you hear that, Nosoi? You can't have my mom! I'm not letting you win!"

Like wax transforming the skin of a dripping candle, Lori's expression shivered, shifted, and became a stranger's.

"*You know us? Mortals do not call us by name. They say we are plague, pestilence, death. How do you know our true title?*"

"I know a lot more than you think. Come out and see."

Like a curious bird, Lori's head twitched from side to side. "*You are strong. Like this one. Stronger even. We sense it in you.*"

"That's right." Eva stood and glared down at the evil infecting her mother. "So let her go. Take me. I can help you. I'll give you more power than she ever could."

"*But with the taking of this one, we will be full. Almost whole. The queen will come. Then our reign will begin. No one will escape the Nosoi. No one will escape this,*" they said, Lori's neck swiveling robotically, "*pandemic.*"

"You don't need her. Let her go!" Panic raged within Eva's chest as she screamed the words.

"*You wish to be the vessel for our queen?*"

"Yes! Anything! Just give me back my mom."

"*The honor is yours, mortal.*" Lori's eyes rolled back, and with a grotesque, full-body contortion, she flopped back against the cushions.

"Stop! Let her go!" Eva pressed her weight against her mother and cradled her head between her hands. "Please." She let the tears spill from her eyes as she pleaded. "Use me instead."

Lori's mouth opened wide and the swarm erupted from her throat. They charged at Eva, and she didn't resist as they forced themselves between her lips.

Oracle! Their word bit at the insides of her ears. *You are with him. The immortal.*

Alek's strong hand squeezed hers. "I'm here, Eva!" His words were a faint echo above the screeching within her head.

His kind trapped our queen. Not again. Never again!

Eva's body spasmed horribly. Heat tore through her chest as the Nosoi clawed their way back to freedom and tore out of the open door. Sobbing and gasping for air, Eva collapsed against her mom.

"Shh, shh. Don't cry. Don't cry. Momma's back. It's quiet. They're gone now," Lori murmured. She raised her arms weakly, trying to hold Eva.

Still crying, Eva rested her head against her mother's damp shoulder. Like a wounded bird, Lori's hand fluttered across her daughter's face. "Shh," she repeated, her voice beginning to fade. "Momma's here…. Momma's here. You'll be fine, honey. Everything will be fine."

Scarlet spray painted Lori's face and chest. Eva couldn't stop the tide of sadness coursing through her as she watched the light begin to dim in her mother's familiar, loving gaze.

"Momma, I'm sorry! I'm so sorry!" Eva sobbed.

"There's nothing to be sorry about. You're here now. You saved me, Eva. You made them leave. We got through it. Just us. Like always." Pink foam flecked Lori's lips as she smiled at her daughter. "If I could have chosen from all the little girls in the world, I would have picked you and only you as my daughter."

Eva choked back more tears and made herself smile. "You're the best mom ever, Lori. I'm glad it was just us."

"Remember that you're stronger than you think you are, Eva. Believe in yourself as much as I've always believed in you." Lori's eyelids started to close.

"Momma, please don't leave me!"

For a moment Lori's eyes opened, and her gaze was clear and calm. "I'll never leave you, Eva. I'll always be right here." Lori's hand trembled as she touched Eva's chest, just over her heart. "I love you, Eva. Always."

Then, with a gentle sigh, Eva's mom breathed her last breath, and her head tilted to rest against her daughter's.

THIRTY

Alek lingered next to Eva while her body trembled. She noiselessly sobbed against her mother's still form. He hadn't lost anyone before, not anyone he cared about, and, unless he and the Oracle failed, he wouldn't lose any of his mothers anytime soon. Even then, he knew he would see them again. After all, if they possessed magic, spirits were free to travel to and from Elysium. Stiffly and awkwardly, he placed his hand between Eva's heaving shoulders and patted the back of her wrinkled shirt.

A hushed yet familiar buzzing drifted into the living room from the open front door, and Alek strained to see out the windows into the front yard.

"Alek!" Wide-eyed, Bridget stood in the open doorway motioning for him to come over. "You have to see this."

Guilt tugged at his stomach as he rubbed Eva's back a few more times before stepping onto the porch.

"Is she okay?" Bridget asked.

"No." He jumped off the edge of the porch and gazed

up at the buzzing swarm hovering above the yard.

"Can't say that's not what I expected." She took a deep, shaky sigh and continued. "I want to be in there with her, but we have to fix this first, right?"

"You are correct."

"*We have called our brethren to us for the arrival of the queen. She is near!*" the scarlet cloud shrieked.

"What will become of your queen with no vessel?" Alek shouted at the undulating cloud.

"*We will take a mortal as we have done for centuries. You will not stop Her. You will not stop the Nosoi.*"

"That's it!" Bridget said, charging to Alek's side. "Hey! Hey, Nosoi!"

Alek grabbed her wildly flailing arms and pinned them to her sides. "I will hurt you if it means keeping you from them," he snarled.

"Direct your bad attitude at them. I have an idea. A way to end this without someone else's mom turning up dead."

"*Do not trouble yourself with these humans. Their species is a scourge upon this realm.*"

Alek loosened his grip, and Bridget leaned in and whispered her strategy.

"Do you think it'll work?" she asked.

"Yes, but it may also end your life."

"Totally worth it. Just don't tell Eva." She charged into the middle of the yard. "You need a vessel for your skeevy queen?" she bellowed at the scarlet swarm. "Use me!"

• • •

Bridget's shouts reached Eva's ears, and she looked around the still living room for her friend. The candles' flames cast pulsating shadows, playing tricks on her vision. Her swollen eyes burned. Time was paralyzed as she stared down at her mother. Worlds of unsaid words and unrealized memories tumbled within her. "Momma." She gingerly extended her hand and smoothed back Lori's hair. "I'm sorry."

Electricity crackled outside, stealing Eva's attention. Bridget's blurry form bounced up and down in the front yard as she shouted, "Hey! I'm right here! I'll be the vessel! Take me! End this!"

"No, Bridget! Not you too!" Eva sprinted out the door, but froze as she came to the edge of the patio.

The threatening cloud of buzzing scarlet specks churned in the air above Bridget while crimson sparks of electricity crackled around them. "*An ally of the Oracle. She will do nicely*," they hissed through the growing winds.

"Eva, you mustn't interfere." Alek grabbed her hand and pulled her into the shadows.

"I have to!"

"Oracle, wait. There is something you don't know."

"I'm not interested in explanations! This plague ripped my mother away from me. I won't let it do the same to Bridget. Don't you understand, Alek? She's the only family I have left." Eva tore her arm away from Alek and bounded off the porch.

"Bridget!" Eva's arms blanketed her best friend. Exhaustion swept over her and she gave in, letting her body sag and her tears leak into Bridget's blonde curls. "Don't do this. Don't offer yourself to them. Please. I can't—I can't lose you too."

Bridget wrapped her arms around Eva and spoke against her ear. "It'll take a lot more than some nasty bug creatures to get rid of me. We're stuck together for the long haul, and I've got a pretty solid plan to destroy these fuckers, so trust me."

Eva pushed away and glared up at the Nosoi. "You hear that? You're not taking her!"

Alek snagged her wrist, forcing her to face him. "Think, Eva! Their numbers have grown. The death of your mom and the others they've killed have made them stronger."

Numbness coated Eva's body as she looked up to see tendrils of scarlet snaking through the sky, all converging above Bridget. "Oh, God, no. They can't be winning."

"They can, and they *will* if you stop Bridget."

"Told you!" Bridget shouted. "And you know how much I love being right."

"I'm ignoring you." Eva held up her hand. "Alek, you have to help me. Bridget doesn't know what she's up against. They'll kill her, Alek. And I'll die too."

"Eva." He lowered his voice, pulling her away from Bridget. "She's your best friend, but she is also the last chance your realm and Tartarus have. You're the Oracle. You must choose."

"But I didn't choose this, and my mom is…" Her voice cracked as she struggled to utter the word. "Dead." Even after she said it, it didn't feel real. Nothing felt real.

"And I am sorry. The Underworld is a powerful realm. You will see her again. I give you my word. Until then, you must face what is happening now, and Bridget does indeed have a plan."

"Will it work?"

"It must. It's our only option."

"But will it work, and will she be safe?"

Alek hesitated.

"Your silence tells me everything. I'm stopping this. And this time, don't pull me away."

Thunder crashed, and the cool fall breeze turned thick and hot as she turned back to Bridget, whose wide-eyed stare was fixed on the converging cloud.

"*The queen is coming! The queen is coming! The queen is coming!*" the Nosoi's shrill, whistling voices chanted emphatically.

"Bridget, I'm not letting you do this!" Eva shouted, but slivers of crackling scarlet lightning engulfed her words.

She rushed to Bridget and grabbed her. Her ivory skin glowed pale pink in the red rays cast down from the sparks of electricity igniting the sky. Eva tugged on Bridget's arm, but the petite blonde remained cemented in place. "What have you done to her?"

"*It is not us. It is the queen. She grows strong. She is coming.*"

Bridget turned her head and rested her gaze on Eva. The glimmer in her eyes had vanished, replaced by thin veins of red. "The queen is here." Bridget's chin pointed to the sky and her arms spread wide, knocking Eva to the ground.

Thunder roared in the heavens and caused the soil under Eva's feet to vibrate. "Alek, do something!"

"This is how it must be," he boomed over the storm.

Eva's hand quivered as she grabbed Alek's and squeezed. "It's going to be okay. There may be a one-in-a-million chance this will work, but I choose to believe in that chance." Hope flared within her. "The good guys will win, and we're the good guys!" Droplets splattered against her shoulders, and Eva cast her glance to the night sky as it bled scarlet rain.

THIRTY-ONE

A beacon of red lit the sky as James sped away from Veronica's, rushing to get as far from the stench of regurgitated seafood as possible. The tip of his sock was wet from where he'd rinsed off his shoe, after Veronica thought her heaving was over and came to sit with him on the couch. Chunks had gone flying, a bit of which landed squarely on the toe of his boot. "First blood and now puke. I have to get rid of these shoes."

James stopped behind the line of cars waiting at the flashing red stoplight. The electricity was out, and even though it was late, which usually meant little traffic, the streets were congested with drivers angry at having to stop at every block to pause at a red light. "Well, shit. At least I made it out of Pierce's office before the power went out." In his experience, companies seemed to always have security glitches when things like this happened, and he hated to think of what would have occurred if he'd still been in that lab when his fellow officers arrived. "Bridget and Eva owe me for that one. Hell, humankind owes me."

He glanced down at his vibrating phone. "Damn." He'd forgotten to text Bridget the good news. Finally there was something they could relax about. There was no reason to worry about the bodies or any samples getting to the CDC. That problem had taken care of itself. Sure, it was disgusting, but it was also no longer a concern.

He plucked his cell out of the cup holder. Bridget had sent him six texts, called him four times, and left one message. "What the fuck?" He pressed the voicemail icon and Bridget's frantic sobs blared through his speakers.

"*James, you have to come now. She's dead. Lori's dead. The Nosoi killed her. It's bad. It's so bad. But I'm going to make them pay. They need a vessel, and when their queen comes, I'm going to be that vessel. I'm going to kill them.*" The message ended as burgundy lightning crashed overhead.

His tires screeched as he flipped a U-turn, then sped toward Eva's and the churning scarlet sky.

• • •

A beam of crimson bathed Bridget as she stood frozen in place under the control of an ancient, infectious evil. Alek replayed the events in his mind and searched for anything he'd missed, anything that could change this scene and destroy the Nosoi without the possible loss of the Oracle's companion. *I have done all I can. This is how it must end.*

A familiar hum tickled Alek's ears, and he cast his gaze to the sky. An onslaught of buzzing red specks poured from the low-hanging clouds and merged with the swarm thrumming over Bridget. United, they pulsed with a deafening purr.

Eva's nails dug into the back of his hand, and the drips of scarlet rain streaming down his skin made it impossible to tell whether or not he was bleeding. He studied the Oracle's profile. Wet hair matted the side of her face, and her lip quivered slightly as she repeated, "It's going to be okay. It's going to be okay."

He opened his mouth to speak, but couldn't think of any words to soothe her. He squeezed her hand and, powerless, watched the swarm converge on Bridget like a flock of deranged swifts. Anger warmed Alek's chest as he watched them disappear into her open mouth. He was supposed to be a warrior, aggressive and courageous. Instead he stood by, watching and waiting for someone else to make a move to save them. This was what had to happen. He knew that, but it didn't stop shame from pooling in his gut.

Thunder roared overhead, and the rose-colored rain ceased as the crimson sky dimmed, replaced by the muted black of night.

Bridget's arms slapped down at her sides, and her head sagged against her chest, but she remained firmly upright.

"Bridge?" Eva called out timidly.

"Wait here. I'll see to her." He reveled in the opportunity to take charge and prove his title of warrior.

The air around Bridget was sweltering. Ripples of heat radiated off of her, drying the beads of red rain streaming down her skin.

"Bridget, do you hear me?" Alek asked. Bridget's only response was the robotic twitching of her fingers. "Eva, I need—"

Tires squealed against the pavement, interrupting him. Alek glanced up as James sprang from his car and rushed to

Bridget's side. "Whoa, it's hot over here. What happened? You didn't let her go through with it, did you?"

"We had no choice," Alek said flatly, annoyed by the sudden appearance of the detective.

"So it's done?" James asked. "You let her offer herself up to those things?"

"As I said, we had no choice," Alek repeated.

"Had no choice my ass. Aren't you supposed to be some big shot hero?"

Alek balled his fists and narrowed his eyes at the detective. "Have you forgotten who stands before you?" he snarled.

"Both of you shut the hell up." Spittle flew from Eva's lips as she punched out the words. "Bridget didn't do this so we could ruin our only chance by fighting each other."

James cleared his throat. "You're right, Eva."

Alek pulled his menacing gaze away from James.

"Alek, finish what you were saying. You need something? What can we do?" Eva asked.

"We must find something to bind her, so she can't escape when she awakens. Then we must take her to the river and end this evil once and for all."

James shook his head. "Wait, you're not submerging Bridget in the river, are you? I knew she had something crazy in mind, but I never thought it'd be this bad."

"This creature is not Bridget, and if we do not kill it, it will destroy your earth. Either join us or take your leave," Alek said.

"I'm in. Of course. But let's not pretend this whole thing doesn't suck. I have handcuffs in my car." James's feet splashed against the shallow puddles dotting the yard as he sprinted to his car.

"Alek, her head is moving. I think she's waking up," Eva said.

He readied himself and stepped closer to the blonde. "Bridget?"

Her hand shot out and grabbed him by the throat. "*I answer to 'Queen,'*" she seethed, her voice echoed by another.

Pain seared his neck and crept up his face. He grabbed her wrist and squeezed. Her bones were so thin. One strong flick of his hand, and they'd shatter under his grip. But he couldn't do that. Not to Bridget, and definitely not in front of Eva. Boils bubbled on his skin, and marched up his arm.

"Don't touch her. The infection will spread to you," he gurgled as James cautiously rejoined them, gripping silver shackles.

"*Mortal.*" She pursed her lips and blew a steady stream of her Nosoi followers into James's face.

Hacking, James tumbled backward.

Bridget's vibrant blue eyes faded, and scarlet orbs took their place. "*How do you end an immortal? Not with plague. I know this all too well. If I crush this pipe you use to breathe, will you emerge healed and renewed?*"

Eva stirred in Alek's periphery vision, and he fought to turn his head to face her.

"*Injure me, Oracle, and you injure your mortal ally,*" the creature within Bridget warned.

"I think she'll get over it." Eva charged the queen with enough force that she lost her grip on Alek. He crumpled to the ground, panting while his immortal gifts took over and cleansed his body.

"*I expected more from you, Oracle.*" Bridget's bubbly

chirp vanished.

Lifting himself from the ground, Alek shouted, "It's done. The queen has cemented her place within Bridget. Detective, the shackles." Alek held out his hand, and James tossed them over. "The Nosoi will lie to you, and fill you with rage. Hold on to what you know is true. We will end this, and you will be well." Alek didn't wait for a response before sprinting to Eva's side.

• • •

Eva had never been in a physical fight before, but it was just as painful as she'd imagined. This fight was even more so, because of the instantaneous sickness delivered with every touch of Bridget's skin.

"*Where is your magic?*" the queen taunted.

"My magic? My magic's right here." Eva locked eyes with Alek, and she didn't need words to know what to do. She balled her fists and leaped into the air, striking Bridget's chin on the way down. Bridget's body locked up and remained rigid as she smacked against the ground. "Hurry and get those cuffs on her," she instructed, shaking out her aching fist. "Man, Bridget's going to be mad at me tomorrow."

Thirty-Two

The rain started up again, and clear droplets beat against the windshield. "What do we do when we get there? Throw her in the water and hope for the best?" James squinted and increased the speed of the windshield wipers.

"No, we'll be there to make sure she's okay," Eva said.

The discomfort clawing at his chest was too much. Spit dotted the steering wheel as he hacked. "To make sure she doesn't drown, you mean?" Anger nipped at his thoughts, and he spoke from between clenched teeth.

Silence blanketed the car as James turned sharply, and Bridget's body rolled around in the trunk.

"She'll be okay," Eva whispered.

Spears of lightning dissected the black, starless sky as James pulled his car into an empty parking lot lining the Arkansas River.

"Get out. This is as close as we get." He leaned out of the open driver's side door and let the coughs overtake him. Blood dripped from his lips and splattered against the pavement.

He met the three of them in the thick, white beams shooting out from the headlights. Rain pelted his skin, and he squinted against the droplets falling from his brow. Confusion and fury spun within him, but he calmed as he examined Bridget's profile. Flashes of light illuminated her delicate features, and the heat pulsing off of her felt like home.

"*I see you.*" She hadn't spoken, but her low purr coursed through him, vibrating his lungs and forcing him to cough into his wet sleeve.

"James! James, are you okay?" Eva shouted through the thunder.

He regained control of his thoughts and nodded apologetically at Eva. They followed the headlight's beams to the steep riverbank. The wide, flat asphalt of the bike path was well cared for, but two yards off of it the underbrush was thick and the footing treacherous. Alek and Eva both clung to Bridget's sagging body. Their hands and arms were swollen and chapped. Thunder roared overhead as James tripped after them down the rocky embankment.

Spider webs of lightning cracked through the clouds and illuminated the sandy river's edge. "Look!" Eva shouted, pointing upriver.

A small wooden canoe bounced atop the surface of the tumultuous water. James barreled the rest of the way down the steep path and ran to the boat. A thin rope tied around a large branch of driftwood held it in place, and he blindly untied the loose knot. He grabbed the boat and guided it down the river.

"Get in!" he yelled, taking out the oars and handing

one to Eva.

"You got her?" she asked Alek, before gripping James's shoulder to steady herself as she climbed into the boat.

Alek lowered Bridget's body into the canoe and turned his attention to James.

"You don't have to say it," James said. "I'm staying here. This is too important, and right now I'm too much of a liability."

Alek nodded in agreement, and waded out into knee-high water before hopping in the boat.

"We need to find the deepest point," Alek said, the muscles in his arms contracting as he pulled the oars through the churning waves. Thunder rumbled overhead, and he let it dissipate before continuing. "There has been a lot of rain, so it should be deep enough out in the middle." The downpour beat against the inside of the boat, creating a puddle around Bridget's body. Tension knotted Alek's shoulders as the boat surged closer to the river's middle. "This place is good enough," Alek boomed over the storm.

Eva released the oar from her shaking grasp and let it slap against the bottom of the boat. "I'm scared."

"This is how it must be. There is nothing to fear." Alek grabbed the rope, and looped it around Bridget's ankle before securing the knot.

"We could kill her." Eva's eyes were wide with equal parts fear and determination.

Water streamed down her face as Alek cupped her soft cheeks in his palms. "I cannot assure you Bridget will survive, but I know that you are strong enough to."

Bridget stirred in the bottom of the boat, tipping it from side to side. "*I will take this mortal with me. End me, return me to Tartarus, and her soul will be lost forever."*

Eva eyes brimmed with tears. "Do it, Alek."

In a final attempt to remain in the Mortal Realm, the queen narrowed her scarlet gaze and released a breath of crimson specks into Alek's face. Keeping his grip on her shirt, he let the small cloud of Nosoi invade his lungs. They made a hasty retreat, and Alek's chest burned as he coughed. Wiping the spit from his lips, he focused his attention on the queen.

"You have no power over us." Alek balanced himself and lifted her into the air. Her feet kicked wildly, and she snarled and gnashed her teeth. "Turn away, Eva." As Eva turned to face the shore, Alek slammed the queen into the water. Bubbles burbled from her open mouth as her face disappeared under the murky waves. Her shackled hands thrashed about above the surface, clawing at the air. The boat jolted as her legs drifted under the hull and she kicked at it violently.

The pride and accomplishment he usually felt when defeating a foe were not present in this victory. Guilt and sorrow seeped into him as he held the woman's fighting body under the water.

"Alek, look." He turned to Eva and looked in the direction she was pointing. A figure cut through the water, heading straight toward them.

"Detective?"

• • •

Confusion swept over James as the Nosoi infiltrated his thoughts, picking them apart and replacing them with their own. Lightning lit the sky, and anger bubbled within his aching chest as he watched Alek submerge Bridget in the river. He tried not to imagine how terrified she must be, how filled with pain and despair. Bridget must be the bravest person he'd ever known, letting that creature inside of her just so the warrior and his Oracle could kill it.

"Don't get angry. You're not thinking clearly. This is okay. They're doing something good." He closed his eyes, no longer willing to watch the snippets of events the lightning afforded him. "A few minutes. That's all it takes. Drowning is fast. You remember. Only a few minutes."

Rain no longer cooled his skin, and the growls of thunder faded as a long-suffocated memory came alive, engulfing him, dragging him into the past. He opened his eyes. Blue Pacific waters and a peaceful Hawaiian sky replaced Tulsa and the muddy Arkansas River.

"Melanie! Somebody help me! Melanie!" He charged into the raging waters and let his body take over. He sliced through the waves, heading toward where he'd last seen her.

By the time he reached her, his arms were on fire, and his chest burned with crippling ferocity. His exhausted legs fought to keep him afloat as he put his arm around her torso.

"Oh, God no. Please no, no, no." His hands trembled wildly as he brushed the wet clumps of hair from her face and parted her pale, blue-tinged lips. He covered her lips with his. Their coolness sent waves of panic down his spine, and he forced air into her lungs. His head slipped under the water, and he struggled to keep above the churning waves. "Someone, help!" he yelled as he emerged. His legs would no longer kick, and he again slipped under the surface. Her mass of tangled hair swept through his fingers as he released his grip on the woman he was willing to trade his life for.

Jay, Mel's whisper slid through the darkness engulfing him. *I'll find you again. Wait for me.*

"No!" Water filled his mouth as he shouted. "We've already found each other. Don't go!"

"James!" Cold wind blew on his back as he was pulled from the water and dropped onto something hard.

"Mel?" he croaked.

The bright, cheery Hawaiian sky shattered as lightning splintered overhead and thunder pummeled his ears. Rain pelted his face, and he recoiled. "Melanie?" He reached over the side and feverishly clawed at the dark water.

"James!"

He turned toward the voice, trying to focus on the person it belonged to.

"Get your shit together." Confusion wrinkled Eva's brow. "I don't know what the hell is going on with you, but we have to save Bridget. Get us back to shore."

"The Nosoi. They—they messed with my head, made me see things." He tried to explain, but Eva was already busy helping Bridget. James grabbed an oar and sliced it through the water. His thoughts spun as he realigned himself with reality. "Mel's gone. She's really gone." He battled the current of the rising Arkansas River. He hadn't been able to save his fiancée, but he couldn't let Bridget down. He wouldn't let Bridget down.

THIRTY-THREE

Bridget had never been so still. Color had drained from her face, except her lips, which were the hue of fresh blueberries. Eva tipped Bridget's chin up and started CPR. "C'mon Bridget," she begged, and pushed against her chest with the heels of her hands. Again, she covered Bridget's cold mouth with hers in a desperate attempt to revive her. "Nothing's happening." She turned to Alek, tears warming her cheeks.

He opened his mouth to say something, but only shook his head, hopelessness dulling his eyes.

Her arms burned as she pounded against Bridget's sternum.

The boat stopped suddenly when they reached the shore, knocking Eva off-balance. She stared down at Bridget, who was still unmoving and pale. Sorrow sucked the air from her chest, and her sobs came out in silent gasps. "Please don't leave me too." She rested her lips against Bridget's cold, wet forehead.

"I wish I could have healed you." While she spoke,

amber smoke poured from her mouth, tickling her tongue as it floated from her to her friend. It caressed Bridget's cheeks before slipping between her parted lips. Eva said a silent prayer to the ancient Oracle she knew was watching.

You do not need me, young Oracle. Your gifts are your own, Pythia purred in response.

A new scarlet streak painted Bridget's blonde hair as her eyelids fluttered open, and her chest expanded. Water dribbled down her chin as she sat up and coughed into her hands. "Did it work?" she asked between breaths.

"You were dead," James and Alek said in unison.

Alek cleared his throat and continued. "The Oracle revived you."

"Good thing you took first aid in school. I thought getting CPR would suck a lot more than that." Bridget fanned her face. "It's hot out here. Is anyone else hot?"

Eva shivered against the wind. "It's probably a little bit of leftover magic. I used one of my powers to heal you."

Bridget squinted up at her. "But you can't heal people."

"Yes, yes I can." Eva couldn't stop grinning. "I don't know exactly how, but I can, and I did." Exuberance filled her cells, and she threw herself against her best friend. "And now you're back, and you can't ever leave me again."

THIRTY-FOUR

James lived in the heart of his jurisdiction, in a drafty rental with creaking floors and chipped paint, but it suited him. Its only purpose was to shield him from the elements while he slept. Well, that had been its only purpose.

The doorbell rang, and he checked his reflection in the TV before answering.

"Hey!" Bridget bounced up and kissed him. Her cinnamon gum left a hint of spice on his lips. "I thought we could stay in tonight and, I don't know, watch Netflix and chill." Her presence brightened the barren space, and almost made him forget about how lonely he'd been. "And since your fridge is always empty, I brought food." She pulled a Tupperware container out of her tote and headed for the kitchen.

Cheesy goodness covered each fat noodle, and his mouth watered at the sight of the homemade meal. "You made this?"

"Well, no. My mom made it, but it was my idea to

bring it over here instead of hoarding it at my place while I watched *The Office* for the millionth time, so you're welcome. Now, go sit down. I'm sure you've had another killer week at work pretending you don't know about what's really been happening."

"You're going to serve me?"

"Only because I know you'll return the favor later." A lascivious smile curled her lips.

Desire warmed his core, but he did as he was told and took a seat on the far end of the couch, where he could still see into the kitchen. He was learning that, with Bridget, it was best to go in fully energized, so he needed the carbs.

"Is this the only silverware you have?" She held up a box of assorted plastic cutlery, and raised an eyebrow.

"Yeah. The real stuff is still in a box somewhere." He motioned to the unlabeled boxes stacked against the wall.

"How long have you lived here?" Plastic clattered against the countertop as she shook out the utensils.

James shrugged. "I don't know. Nine months maybe."

"Women grow an entire human being in nine months, and you haven't even finished unpacking."

He smiled. "Think of it as art."

Bridget's alarm blared, and she squealed excitedly and clapped her hands. "The news is starting! Turn it to channel six." She plopped down on the couch and handed James a steaming bowl of macaroni.

He balanced the savory dish and fished the remote out from between the couch cushions. "I thought you hated watching the news."

"I can grow and mature and stuff," she said through a mouthful of cheesy pasta. "Plus, a crew came into the store and interviewed me about shopping local. The segment airs tonight and I want to watch myself."

James changed the channel, and let Bridget settle against him before taking his first bite.

"The effects of the midtown Tulsa power outage and deadly viral outbreak are still being felt throughout our city. Local pharmacies are already out of the flu vaccine, and many Oklahomans are left wondering what will happen to them if another outbreak occurs."

"If people only knew what really happened," James mumbled. "You should hear what Schilling's saying. He's not a conspiracy nut or anything, but all of this might just tip him over."

"I don't think he or anyone else would believe what went down, even if you convinced Alek and Eva to show off their abilities. You saw it with your own eyes and still had trouble believing me."

"Yeah, but I've grown and matured and stuff since then." He winked. "Where are Eva and Boy Wonder anyway?"

"Alek took her to Ely." Bridget paused and scrunched her face. "Elo? Eluh? Heaven. Alek took Eva to the Underworld's version of heaven to visit her mom."

"That's great. Someone dying suddenly like that can really mess a person up," James said.

"I'm so glad she gets to go see her. She can't stay long, but it's better than nothing. Oh, look! It's me!"

"And don't you look good." He smiled.

"Shh! It's me. We have to listen." Bridget turned up the volume and nestled against him.

James chuckled softly to himself.

What they were doing was simple, and it made him

realize he'd been living all wrong. *Mel isn't coming back.* That was something he'd known, but his heart hadn't felt it until that night at the river. *I'm done telling myself I can't be happy because it will betray Mel.* He could be happy again, and Bridget and his new circle of friends proved it was possible.

Hell, maybe he'd even finish unpacking.

• • •

Electricity crackled in the air as the deepest level of the Underworld formed around Eva. She ignored the static lifting the hairs on her arms and followed Alek into the Hall of Echoes. Soft gold light illuminated brilliant turquoise pools rippling up from the shimmering floor.

Eva gasped. "What happened? This is all so beautiful."

"We defeated the queen of the Nosoi and returned the escaped to their rightful place. Tartarus is repairing itself. But that is not why we're here." Alek nodded over her shoulder.

"Mom?"

"Eva! Oh, my girl—my precious girl!"

Eva rushed to her mother, tears welling in her eyes. She wanted to hurl herself into her mom's arms, but Lori had taken a small step back. "Momma?"

"It's okay honey, but you shouldn't touch me."

Tentatively, Eva reached for her mom's familiar hand, and sparks shot from her fingertips. "What's wrong? Why can't I touch you?" Tears spilled down Eva's cheeks.

"I'm not really here, Eva. My soul is in Elysium. The Furies used their magic so I could see you."

"You know about the Furies?" Eva asked.

"I know about it all."

"I'm sorry. I should have told you everything."

"As your mother I'd say yes, you should have. As a rational human being, I'm pretty sure had you told me about all of this," Lori paused, making a gesture that took in Alek and the turquoise pools surrounding them, "I would have insisted you check yourself into the psych ward at Laureate."

"And now?"

"Well, there's nothing like dying and then waking up in Elysium to broaden your horizons." A smile brightened Lori's eyes. "I know everything—everything about Alek and Pythia. I'm so proud, Eva. I'm so proud of you."

"Thanks Mom. It's such a relief that you know." Eva struggled against the need to touch her mom, to curl up in her arms and sob with relief, like she was a kid again. "But what about you? Is Elysium nice?"

Lori's smile widened. "Nice? It's better than nice. Did you know that, in Elysium, I can drink all the wine I want and not get a hangover?"

"Really, that sounds—"

"And we feast. Every day, Eva. Every single day. *Without gaining weight*," Lori said, sotto voice.

Eva grinned at her mom. Sure, she looked a little insubstantial and blue, and she was wearing a draped, silky dress that was disconcertingly see-through, but she definitely looked good. "That's great Mom. And I swear you look thirty."

Lori giggled. "I know, right?"

Alek clear his throat, drawing their attention. "Eva, your mother's immortal soul is now anchored to Elysium. She has been granted the ability to visit you here in Tartarus, but even the Furies cannot change the natural order of things, and her visits must be short."

"She has to go? Now?" Loneliness rushed over her at the thought of losing her mom again.

"It's okay honey. I can come back. It'll be like you actually went away to college and we're Skyping. But before I go, I have to hear what's been going on since you banished that plague." Lori sat at the edge of one of the turquoise pools and patted the space next to her.

Eva sat beside the ethereal being that was her mom. As she spoke, she felt herself relaxing into the familiar security of talking, just like she used to before the Underworld and Oracles and ancient evils got in the way. "Well, you'll be happy to know that I'm no longer wanted by the police. Turns out, there was zero evidence against me, which completely makes sense since I didn't do anything wrong. Alek, on the other hand, is a totally different case. But I'm pretty sure he doesn't have anything to worry about. They're never going to be able to find him, especially since we now have a detective on our team, and he's also dating Bridget."

Lori frowned. "You know I love Bridge, but I wouldn't count on her love life to save the day." She glanced at Alek, who was standing close beside Eva. "I'd count on Alek, though. And you. *Mostly you,* Eva." She glanced at Alek, "No offense. Your mothers have told me all about you, and I do appreciate that you are Eva's warrior, but I think my daughter has smarts and strengths that go beyond even an immortal's comprehension."

Alek smiled at Lori. "No offense taken. I agree with you. I have her back, but she's the Oracle."

Lori turned her gaze to Eva. Slowly, she lifted her translucent hand, as if to caress her daughter's cheek. "Oh

Alek, she's so much more than that." Then she looked up at Alek and smiled knowingly. "But I think you might already understand that. Take care of my girl, Alek."

And then Lori's body began to shimmer.

"Momma?"

"Don't worry honey. We'll talk again soon. I love you. I'll always love you."

"I love you, too!" Eva called, as her mom's body faded away.

"Come here, Eva," Alek said.

Eva let him take her into his arms, where she cried a mixture of happy and sad tears.

THIRTY-FIVE

Eva hurried around her house, tidying up before Alek magically materialized in her living room for their first official date.

"So, you're going on a date with Warrior Boy. You excited?" Bridget's voice chimed through the phone.

"Yes, I'm excited. Nervous, actually. My hands are all sweaty." She pressed the phone between her shoulder and her ear, carrying an armful of unfolded clothes into the laundry room and tossing them back into the dryer.

"You shouldn't be nervous. He's already seen you looking drowned-rat horrible."

Eva cringed at the thought. "But this is a *date* date. Way different than frantically running around trying to save the world."

"True, but I'm sure you guys will have the best time. You're practically made for each other. Now, for the important questions. One: what are you wearing? And two: do you think you'll finally have sex with the man?"

"I don't know what I'm wearing." She flipped on the bathroom light and frowned at the reflection of her in pajama pants and a baggie sweatshirt. "I haven't gotten dressed yet. And I'm not answering your second question."

"Stop being such a prude. I saw him on top of you on my couch, remember?"

Eva's cheeks warmed with the memory. "Bridge, I really have to go. He'll be here any minute."

"Fine," Bridget huffed. "Call me tomorrow. I expect to get all the juicy details."

Eva hung up the phone and tossed it on her bed. It started blaring the second it hit the comforter.

She answered it without checking the caller ID. "Bridget, I really can't talk to you right now. I still have a million things to do before he gets here."

"Eva?" Through the crackling reception, she detected a faint hint of familiarity.

"Yeah. Who is this?"

"Eva, it's me. It's your father."

THE END.... FOR NOW.

ACKNOWLEDGEMENTS

No one. I did it all myself!

But seriously, there is a team of people supporting, inspiring, and assisting me along the way.

Randall, you were sent from the heavens. Thank you for teaching me, inspiring me, and helping me to become a kickass author.

My Diversion Books family—I think our plan to take over the world is coming along very nicely. Muahahahaha!

Ja! Mommy, baby forever!

To Scott Sigler, Neil Gaiman, Jennifer Armentrout, Kresley Cole, Gena Showalter and all the other amazing authors whose books I live to read, I find motivation on every page. Thank you.

To you, the readers! If I could come off this page and kiss you right on the mouth, I would. Thank you for your continued support. And remember, be kind to yourself.

Kristin Cast is a *NY Times* and *USA Today* bestselling author who teamed with her mother to write the wildly successful House of Night series. She has editorial credits, a thriving t-shirt line, and a passion for all things paranormal. When away from her writing desk, Kristin loves relaxing with her significant other and their dogs, and discovering new hobbies. This year she'll work on swimming, yoga, and adding to her *Doctor Who* collection.